FALL BACK

RILEY FLYNN
MIKE WOLFE

SYNDICATE PRESS

FALL BACK

It's not the end.
The Apocalypse is only just beginning...

The Eko virus sweeps the globe in mere days, killing billions. Air Force One disintegrates in a ball of flame. The Secretary of Defense holds a pistol to the head of an Army grunt. The world has gone insane. And the apocalypse is just getting warmed up.

Echo Company is woken in the middle of the night and put on the last plane out of Germany. They might be the last special forces operators anywhere in the world. They're used to being the men who go bump in the night. But now they're all that stands between society and absolute chaos.

Captain Jax Booth never planned on being a father. Not yet, anyway. But the Eko virus killed the woman he loved, and left him to care for her daughter in a world that was falling apart. So he did what he had to. He got Hayley to Cheyenne Mountain, the last bastion of safety anywhere in the world. If there's one thing the Eko virus can't get through, it's 500 feet of reinforced rock...

In time, the virus burns itself out. A small band of survivors establish themselves in the Rockies, and finally pause for breath. The virus might be gone, but winter is coming. It's time to rebuild. To scavenge. To hunt.

To survive.

PROLOGUE

AIR FORCE ONE, SOMEWHERE OVER NEVADA

The red light on the camera across from his desk stared at him like an accusing eye. *This is your fault*, it said. *The buck stops here. It says so right on your desk.*

He shook his head and cleared his throat just as another riot of turbulence rocked the 747. Even the air was against him now, it seemed—the flight had been rocky ever since they took off from Edwards Air Force Base less than an hour earlier, destination Colorado.

A screen above the red light showed him his own face in real time: the relief map of lines and crevices that had burrowed their way across his features over the past eight years, the slicked-back hair that had changed inexorably from chestnut to silver. He'd read once that all presidents who weren't gray when they took office had gone gray over the course of their terms. Except Reagan, of course, but he routinely lied about dying his hair.

Terrence Fletcher had never lied to the American public about his hair. All he'd lied about was the impending doom of the nation whose citizens had put him in the Oval Office not once but twice, and really, it was more a lie of omission.

Keep telling yourself that, he thought bleakly as he stared into his own haunted eyes. *It'll make it easier to tell the biggest lie in the history of this great nation: that everything's going to be okay.*

He watched the eyes on the screen widen as a sharp rap on the door sent a shock of adrenaline through him. He was more on edge than he would have believed possible even just a few hours ago.

"Come," he called, straightening his tie. Outside the window beside his desk, he saw the comforting lights of the F-35 Eagle escort in the night sky. Its twin was on the other side of the plane.

The door opened a crack to reveal the face of a White House intern, the mousy girl with huge glasses. AF1 had taken off with a skeleton staff, including this girl, whose name Fletcher could never remember.

"Mr. President?" she squeaked. "Can I—I mean, are you—"

"You're not interrupting me," he said gently. "What can I do for you?"

She gripped her clipboard to her chest like a shield. "Mr. Fredericks says the satellite link with the networks is finally up. They're ready to broadcast your message."

Fletcher nodded and sighed deeply.

"All right, send him in. Let's get this over with."

A portly middle-aged man squeezed past the intern and entered the office. He nodded to dismiss the girl, who gave Fletcher a pleading glance before the door closed on her. It was only a fraction of a second, but that look was enough to make the president's guts go cold.

Jerry Fredericks dropped a sheaf of papers on the desk. His cheeks glowed red as they always did when he was under stress.

"It's that bad, huh Jer?" Fletcher asked quietly.

Fredericks had the worst poker face of anyone Terrence Fletcher had ever known. It had made him easy to fleece in games back in their UCLA days, but it had been an asset in his role as press secretary. Until shit had started to go sideways. These days reporters looked at him with a mix of distrust and pity.

He ran a hand through his thinning hair. "The cascade effect has increased exponentially over the last twenty-four hours," he said shakily. "That's why we're hitting so much turbulence; the pilots are only getting sketchy signals from the ground."

"I figured that was it." Fletcher nodded. "And there's no end in sight?"

"That's just it, sir: the end *is* in sight."

The bleak look on the man's face told Fletcher all he needed to know.

"Then this is it," he sighed. "How long?"

"Intel from the NSA's special task force says the Eastern Seaboard will likely be completely dark in less than a week. It'll move westward from there. The continental U.S. has ten days at the most."

Fletcher stuck a hand in his pants pocket and gave his scrotum a hard flick. The sharp pain confirmed that he wasn't asleep, and this wasn't a nightmare. This was happening. As if sensing what he'd just done, Fredericks put a hand on the president's shoulder.

"It gets worse, sir," he said quietly. "Are you ready?"

Fletcher nodded, eyes on the stack of papers on the desk.

"Eko's initial mortality rate is confirmed at 98.9 percent. CDC estimates less than four percent of the population has been inoculated at this point, and we're about to lose the means of production for the vaccine. The last truckloads of X-57 have already arrived at strategic points."

"Strategic points!" Fletcher barked a harsh laugh. "Let's shitcan the euphemisms, okay, Jer? I think we're long past being able to sugarcoat this. The last of the vaccine is going to military personnel. American citizens are out in the cold. Literally. And they barely know anything about the cyber attack yet."

Fredericks shrugged. The blotches on his plump cheeks had spread down to his throat.

"I'm sorry," said Fletcher. "I don't mean to shoot the messenger. Especially not you."

"Comes with the job," Fredericks said, managing a weak smile.

The two men looked at each other for a long moment. Fletcher thought those nights playing poker in their dorm room seemed as far away as a star in the night sky right now.

The red light still glared at him from across the room, reminding him that the clock was ticking; they had no idea how long they would be able to broadcast. It was time to lie to the American public. Assuming they were even able to receive the signal at all—there was no guarantee the message would even get through.

"All right," Fletcher said, taking his seat. "Just let me give your speech a once-over and we'll get started."

Fredericks picked up a remote control from on top of a box next to the video screen.

"Ready when you are, sir," he said.

"I think we can shitcan the 'sir' at this point, too," said Fletcher. "Terry and Jerry, still together after all these years. Who would've believed this is how it would all end?"

~

My fellow Americans, it is with the heaviest of hearts that I address you this evening.

As you no doubt are aware, our nation is currently facing a crisis of historic proportions. Many of you have already been forced to watch loved ones suffer through the effects of the Eko virus; perhaps you're even suffering from it yourself. Our experts believe this to be the worst global viral outbreak since the flu pandemic that followed the end of the First World War, and we must steel ourselves for similar results.

Our hospitals are overwhelmed with new cases, and our front-line people are doing everything they can to treat the sick and ensure the virus is contained as well as it possibly can be.

This outbreak would challenge the resources of even the strongest of nations on its own. But at the same time, America's electronic infrastructure has been attacked by an enemy state. You have likely already seen the results of this in the form of rolling electrical blackouts and spotty reception with your communications devices. Simply put, things just don't work as well as they used to.

Worse, we have seen evidence that the effects of this attack have begun to spread globally. This means our communications with our allies have become less than reliable, and relationships with a number of foreign powers that wish us harm have been seriously destabilized.

Under our current circumstances, America is, unfortunately, unable to continue functioning as a civilian-led society. Therefore, this administration is ordering a military intervention on the advice of the FAA, FEMA, and other government departments. We have thought long and hard about this course of action and—ahem, excuse me, I have a frog in my throat—we can see no alternative. We must plan for the future, a future in which America the bold, the brave, and the free continues in the strongest possible fashion.

Oh, for Christ's sake. Let's speak the truth here: America is now officially under martial law. I wish to God we had another alternative, but we don't. What? I know I'm off script, Jerry. I don't care.

My fellow Americans, even if you've never listened to me in the past eight years, even if you didn't vote for me and you think I'm a complete idiot, or an asshole or a traitor, or everything else they call me on social media, I beg you to listen to me now: the National Guard is now under federal control and will soon be deployed en masse throughout the streets of America. They will *be armed.*

You can stop with the hand gestures, Jerry, I'm not going to sugarcoat this.

As of this moment, all American civilians are under a strict curfew. This applies to all citizens outside of those directly involved in military, police, health care and first responder business. All leave for these essential personnel is hereby cancelled indefinitely by executive order.

What does this mean for you citizens listening to me right now? Simple: stay home. Lock your door and stay inside. Please don't call the police—they're incredibly busy. Alongside their compatriots in the National Guard, they are the front line in keeping order during these trying times, and they need your respect and cooperation. Once order is restored and the crisis has passed, I give you my word that life will *return to normal.*

I implore you, my friends, to stay safe. This is only temporary. We will not be defeated. This is a disease and, it seems to me, something against which we can fight.

But we will not win this battle at the end of a sword, or down the barrel of a rifle. We will triumph through our social graces, our common sense, and our innate greatness. We must work together to stop the spread of this dreadful plague. We must deliver ourselves from the danger. We must entrust unto ourselves the power to conquer this terrible threat. Good night, and God bless.

~

Fredericks's legs wobbled under him as another shock of turbulence hit the jet. Thank God it hadn't interrupted the recording of the message, Fletcher thought. Even as it was, no one on board could be sure how much of the transmission had actually made it to the other end to be broadcast.

"I apologize for that, Jerry," he said as he rose and tugged the tie loose from his collar. "I didn't want my final message to the American people to be a *total* lie. They deserved to know what was going to start happening around them."

Fredericks nodded. "I wasn't sure how far you wanted to go."

"Even with them knowing that the National Guard is coming, there's going to be armed resistance. But I had to do what I could to try to lessen it. I mean, everything from this point on is a Hail Mary, right?" He snorted a chuckle. "Terry and Jerry and their Hail Marys."

"You gave them hope," said Fredericks. "That's all any president could possibly do under the circumstances."

Fletcher shook his head. Much of his seven years in office had been spent repairing relationships with what seemed like half the goddamn globe, and earning the trust of the American people at a time when the nation's economy was struggling while China's was surging.

And then in the last month, fate chose him as the one president out of forty-six who got to oversee the collapse of the republic. He was responsible for giving people hope in a hopeless situation.

"They're too smart for that," he said. "The time for self-delusion is over."

Another rap at the door. The intern poked her head in, eyes wide behind her glasses. Behind her, Fletcher could hear the rest pf the staff talking frantically.

"B-beg your pardon, sir," she stammered. "Secretary Chase is, um, waiting to speak to you. He said it's urgent."

Fletcher pinched the bridge of his nose. What *wasn't* urgent right now?

"Put him through." He turned to Fredericks. "Take notes. He probably has an update on the deployment of the Guard."

At that moment, a lanky black man with a weathered face and a fringe of white hair around his skull appeared on the screen. He wore a gray suit that looked a size too big for him. Behind him, the walls of the room were also gray, stark and unadorned. He was at Cheyenne Mountain Complex, where Air Force One was currently headed.

"Mr. President," the man said with a nod.

"Marcus. What's happening?"

Chase's gaze flitted to Fredericks. "Can we have the room, Jerry?"

Fredericks glanced at Fletcher, who nodded. "See if you can get those people out there to calm down, will you?"

The press secretary returned the nod. Another wave of frantic noise wafted into the office as the door opened and closed behind him.

Fletcher folded his arms over his chest and propped his butt against the corner of his desk. "All right, Marcus, what's so hush-hush that Jerry can't hear it?"

Chase had a good fifteen years on Fletcher, and all of them showed on his haggard face right now. As if their current situation wasn't bleak enough, the man had been battling brain cancer for the last three months. He'd assured his commander-in-chief when he was diagnosed that he was still able to do his job, and Fletcher hadn't argued. Then, as the events of the last couple of weeks unfolded, it had become imperative to keep Chase in his job.

"I saw the broadcast, Terry," the older man said quietly. "You shouldn't have worded it the way you did. That part about the point of the sword and the barrel of the rifle."

Fletcher bristled. He'd given his cabinet free rein to criticize him when he appointed them—it was a tactic he'd borrowed from Lincoln—but he didn't like Chase's tone or familiarity, even if he was one of the most decorated military men in U.S. history. Fletcher himself had never served.

"Duly noted," he said evenly. "Is that all? I've got a lot to do and miles to go before I sleep."

Chase sighed deeply; Fletcher thought he'd never seen the man look so exhausted.

"Fewer miles than you might think," said Chase.

"What's that supposed to mean?"

"Look out the window."

Fletcher turned his head to the left toward the bank of windows that lined the left wall of his office. His guts clenched as he watched the lights of the Eagle rapidly disappearing into the inky night sky.

"What the hell is going on, Marcus?" he barked. "Did you order my escort away?"

"Yes," said Chase. "I owe you the truth, Terry. And, to be honest, I still held out a glimmer of hope for you up until that speech. But now I realize you're just not a team player. I should have admitted it to myself sooner—you're never going to be on board with this."

"On board with what?" Fletcher's alarm was slowly creeping its way toward panic. "This is your commander-in-chief speaking. Send those fighters back *now*."

On the screen, he watched Chase stand and shamble his way to the door behind him. He flipped the deadbolt, locking the room, then returned to his seat in front of the camera.

"We don't have a lot of time," Chase said. "I imagine the Secret Service people outside your office are already trying to reach the joint chiefs about the escort. They'll put two and two together soon enough—it happened within minutes of me calling you, after all, how could they not—which means they'll be coming for me soon."

The world tilted under Fletcher as if the jet had hit another pocket of turbulence. His felt his face twist, but whether it was in fear or fury, he'd never know.

"What the fuck is going on here?!" he snapped. "You better answer me right now, Chase, or I swear to God you'll be in a cell in Leavenworth by morning."

Chase tented his fingers under his chin and tilted his head to the side.

"I'll be in a cell soon enough," he sighed. "But it'll be here in Cheyenne Mountain. This is where I'll die. For what it's worth, I'm sorry it had to turn out this way."

Before Fletcher could answer, he caught the flicker of lights outside the office window again. They grew larger as a pair of aircraft approached the jet from the northeast, and he felt a wave of relief at the sight of them. The situation was under control again.

He turned his attention back to the man on the screen and saw just how much of a shell Chase had become over the past few months. The toll of his illness seemed to suddenly crush the man.

"Look, Marcus," said Fletcher. "I understand that you're tired, and you're probably not thinking right. Why don't you get yourself down to the infirmary? At the very least they should be able to make you more comfortable. I'll get Benton to take over—"

Chase gave him a weak smile. "You think this is the tumor," he said. "Afraid not. I'm thinking more clearly than I have in my entire life. I just wish you were, too. But it's too late for either of us to turn back now."

Fletcher frowned. That cold sensation in his guts was back, stronger this time.

"What are you talking about, Marcus?" His voice sounded weak in his own ears.

"Those aren't your Eagles, Terry. They're a new experimental drone. Each one is carrying four Swedish Meteor missiles, which are popular among a number of rogue states right now. The drones will be destroyed by the launch, of course, just in case anyone ever has the opportunity to investigate, which I highly doubt. We'll be lucky if we can still get a plane off the ground when this is all over."

At that moment, the office door burst inwards and slammed against the wall behind it, followed by four men with black suits and severe haircuts.

"THAT'S NOT THE ESCORT!" the one in front hollered as the Secret Service agents threw themselves on top of Fletcher, almost crushing him against the sofa on the window wall.

As the fuselage erupted in a flash of orange and yellow and red, Terence Fletcher's last thoughts weren't of his wife or children, or even what was happening around him. They were of Jerry Fredericks, and staying up all night drinking beer and playing poker so many years ago, when the future was still a dream instead of the nightmare it had become.

1

Five Days Earlier – Boblingen, Germany

He only sees her from behind, the flowing black hair draped over her shoulders as they walk through the cobblestone street. It's a quaint little shopping block lined with old Tudor-style buildings, the place where he took her on their first date.

Her feet kick up little puffs of dust with each step. Everything seems so gray on the empty street. Even the air seems gray.

Why won't she turn around?

"It's time," she whispers, but he still can't see her face.

Time? No, not yet. They have loads of time, tons of time. They have their whole lives ahead of them.

He suddenly notices that they're alone on the street, and that she's in her scrubs, the gray ones she wears with a long-sleeved sweater underneath because there's always a bit of a chill in the old hospice where she works.

No, wait—she works at the hospital. Why did I say hospice?

She's shuffling ahead of him down a gray hallway. He hates this place; it's old and claustrophobic, and it smells. It can't be the hospital—that building is new and modern-looking and open. She doesn't work here.

Vague realization starts to set in at the edges of his consciousness, and with it comes a growing alarm that he can feel but doesn't understand.

"Why are we here?" he asks, but as soon as the words are out of his mouth, he knows he doesn't want to hear the answer. He puts his fingers in his ears and shakes his head like a child. No. Nonononono.

She stops in front of him and finally turns to face him. His heartbeat starts to gallop, and suddenly he doesn't want to see her face. No. Not at all. Nonononono.

But his eyes won't close—they're stuck fast to the turning head in front of him. Every moment seems to take a lifetime as his heart pounds in his chest. He knows what he's going to see, but he refuses to accept it. If he doesn't see it, it's not real.

"I'm sorry," she whispers, and the words hit him like an ice pick to the belly. The sound of his own racing breath seems to envelop him as her face finally becomes clear: horribly, horrifyingly clear.

All trace of her former beauty has been painted over by the grayness of the disease. The light in her eyes is now out, replaced by a pair of dead charcoal embers floating above her ravaged cheeks.

NonononononoNO!

"Promise me," she whispers. "I need you to promise."

"I promise," he says through numb lips, not knowing what he's agreeing to. All he's aware of is the growing hole in the center of him throbbing like the dull ache of an infected tooth.

Her smile is hideous on that gray, empty face.

"I love you," he whispers as she recedes into the distance of the hallway, now as long as a football field, a distance he knows he can't cover even if he sprints with everything he has. She's lost to him. He understands that now with an icy clarity that makes his heart crack.

"Jax," she says, but it's not her voice. "Jax, open up, man."

Jackson Booth's eyes snapped open as his hand reflexively reached for a weapon that wasn't there. His heart was still thundering in his chest like a race horse, his face glistening with sweat.

Taptaptap at the door again. He looked around him: he was in the cheap old hotel room he'd rented for the last three weeks. He'd fallen asleep in the chair in the corner. The bunched muscles in his lower back were screaming blue murder. On the single bed next to the latticed window was a girl lying in a lump under the covers, eyes closed, breathing deeply.

Hayley, he told himself. It was Hayley. But that meant...

Rachel. Oh, God, Rachel, no. Nonononono.

Realization flooded into him, bringing with it the wave of grief that had been startled out of him when he woke up.

"Jax," a familiar voice called from the hallway. "Seriously, dude, get up. We gotta move. Orders."

He ignored the pain in his back and leapt to his feet, instinct telling him to let the man in before the noise woke the sleeping girl. He opened the door to see a wide brown face with an annoyed look on it.

"Why you don't answer the door, man?" Ruben Lambert asked as he stepped into the room. "You got a lady in here?"

Jax frowned and brought an index finger to his lips, pointing the other toward the bed.

"Shit," Ruben whispered as he saw the girl. "Sorry, didn't know. What's she doing here?"

Jax was silent, but the look on his face spoke volumes. His friend looked to the girl, then back to him, then back to the girl.

"Aw, no," Ruben moaned, his eyes closing. "Tell me it's not that."

Jackson Booth wasn't the crying sort. He carried his pain inside, like all the men in his family, for better or worse. But he couldn't keep it out of his voice.

"Two-thirty this morning," he husked. "Wasn't time to get her from the hospice to the hospital. Not that there would have been any point by then. After both eyes went gray, they knew it was just a matter of time."

Ruben had no such problems showing emotion; tears shone in his eyes as he draped an arm around Jax's broad neck, stooping a bit to match his friend's height and pulling him close.

"That's fucked up, buddy," he said. "I'm so sorry."

Jax nodded silently. He was glad Ruben was here, even if he didn't show it. They didn't have to say things out loud. They'd been best friends since they met in basic training a dozen years ago. More than brothers in arms, Ruben was his brother in every sense except genetically. Their difference in rank—Jax was a captain, Ruben a chief warrant officer—was something they just worked around.

The two men glanced over at the girl. She was moving fitfully in her sleep, rubbing at her eyes with tiny fists, her long blond hair draped over her face. Her stuffed panda doll—a skinny, bedraggled thing that looked like it had been left out in the elements for a year or so—was held captive in the crook of her arm. Jax hoped her dreams were better than his, but deep down, he knew they weren't. If anything, they were worse.

"Eight years old," Ruben said with a shake of his head. "Ain't right, man. No kid should be an orphan at that age."

He would know, Jax thought. Ruben Lambert had grown up in the foster system in East Los Angeles, shuttled from one home to another every few months for most of his childhood. Signing up on his eighteenth birthday had been a foregone conclusion since he was old enough to understand what the army was.

"So what's going to happen to her?" Ruben asked. "She have any family here in Germany?"

Jax shook his head. "Rachel's parents are in Virginia."

"What about her birth father's folks?"

"They cut off contact with Rachel and Hayley after he died. She never went into detail about it. I guess grief can mess with a person's head."

"Yeah. Or maybe they're just assholes."

"Maybe. Either way, they're out of the picture."

It finally registered in Jax's mind that Ruben was in his fatigues. Behind him, he could see his friend's pea-green duffel in the hallway through the open door.

"What's going on?" he asked. "Why are you here?"

Ruben's eyes widened. "Shit, I forgot," he said, his voice rising before he caught himself and dropped back to a whisper. "Echo

Company's been ordered stateside. Special Ops Command chartered a civilian flight to Colorado Springs. No details, just said to rendezvous at Stuttgart Airport at 1200 hours or face court-martial. I tried to call you, but your phone kept going straight to voicemail."

Jax scowled at the black rectangle of metal and glass lying on the nightstand. "Sorry. Chinese piece of shit won't hold a charge. Did you say a civilian flight?"

"Yeah, don't know what the deal is. I figured you'd gone to see Rachel and came back here. We gotta go, man. From the sounds of things, even bereavement leave is off the table. What're we going to do about Hayley?"

At the sound of her whispered name, the girl stirred under the blankets and let out a sleepy groan. Jax knew he was about to face one of the toughest challenges of his life. He had plenty of experience fighting terrorists, but precious little dealing with children. Rachel had made it clear when Jax first asked her out that she wasn't going to introduce him to Hayley for a while. She didn't say it in so many words, but Jax knew she meant her daughter would only meet someone who was husband material.

They'd fallen madly for each other in just a few months, and Jax had met Hayley in early summer. Things were magical for a couple of months. Then Rachel started showing symptoms of an unidentified virus. As an emergency room nurse, she'd been on the front lines of the outbreak, and was one of the first to be infected, weeks before the virus had been properly identified.

And she was one of the first to die, he thought, swallowing hard.

"Hayley's coming with me," he said.

Ruben's eyebrows rose. "You think Archer will go for that?"

Jax had known Lt. Col. Henry Archer, the commanding officer of 1st Battalion of the 10th Special Forces Group, for almost eight years. He was a decent, fair commander, but Jax bringing a civilian back to the U.S. on a military transport would likely be pushing some boundaries.

"Have comms gotten any better?" he asked. Over the past few days, some sort of computer hack had done significant damage to communications systems throughout the military. Rachel's illness had kept him from paying much attention to it.

"Nah," said Ruben. "If anything, they're worse than ever—wi-fi's been down for three days. I can't connect on my mobile, either. Probably no hope of finding Hayley's grandparents online anytime soon."

"What about internal systems?"

"Not much better. Tons of bugs, from what I hear. Shit's going sideways, and I wouldn't be surprised if this deployment back home is connected to it somehow."

Jax turned to the bed to see Hayley's deep brown eyes looking at him sleepily. They were still red-rimmed from the night before, and it made his heart ache all over again.

"I'll tell Archer I'm her legal guardian," he said.

Ruben cocked an eyebrow. "Since when?"

"Since right now. I'll say we couldn't get the paperwork issued because of the tech glitches. There's no way they can check it before we fly out."

"That's a pretty big gamble, Jax."

"What choice do I have?"

Suddenly Hayley was up and out of the bed, still in the clothes she'd worn to the hospice the night before, and Jax realized she'd been listening to them. She stumbled toward the two soldiers, panic etched into her tiny face, and gripped Jax's arm fiercely.

"Don't leave me here," she pleaded in a papery voice. "Please, Jax, don't leave me alone."

The desolation in her eyes almost made him crack, but he swallowed it down into the dungeon where he kept all his pain under lock and key. With Rachel gone, he was all the girl had, at least until they got back to the States. He lifted her with one arm as if she weighed nothing, and she wrapped her arms around his neck. He felt the soft fabric of her panda doll against the sandpaper skin of his cheek.

"I won't leave you," he whispered into her hair, thinking of Rachel's final, fading words. "I'll never leave you. I promise."

2

Jax scanned the terminal from his vantage point in line, taking in the barely controlled chaos. There were army personnel and support staff milling about that he knew from his two years in Germany, along with others whose faces he recognized. Most of the men and women of Echo Company, the people under his command, sat on their duffels, stripped down to their T-shirts and talking animatedly among themselves. As they did, four young women in scrubs and surgical masks circled around the waiting area like bees, administering needles to everyone who got their boarding passes.

Jax also saw a dozen or so military people milling around, ones who weren't associated with Echo but were in the 1st Battalion, the European arm of the U.S. Special Forces that was based around Stuttgart. He could see now why they were chartering a civilian flight: even a Hercules couldn't transport this many people in a single flight. But why did they all have to be stateside at the same time? What was the hurry?

He looked down at Hayley as they waited to check in. She was scanning the airport as well, probably wondering the same thing he was: where were all the civilians? Outside of Echo and the others he recognized, there were only a handful of people anywhere. Some frantic-looking security folks jogged past every few minutes, but as for other passengers, there seemed to be none.

The girl reached out and squeezed his hand. Hers felt small and cold.

"What is it?" he asked.

She pointed to the clerk checking in the personnel. Jax didn't recognize him; couldn't, in fact, tell anything more about him than the fact he was in fatigues like the rest of them. Other than that, there was nothing to identify him by name or rank.

"That's the guy I talk to?" she whispered.

Jax dropped to one knee so he could be at eye level with her. "Only if he asks you any questions. I'm going to try to make it so that he doesn't, but if he does, what do you say?"

"That you're my guardian and you're taking me back to live with my grandparents."

"Perfect." He held up a palm for a high-five. She slapped it half-heartedly with her panda. Normally it hid away under her pillow until bedtime, but she hadn't let go of it since she'd left the bed in the hotel room that morning.

She had talked about her grandparents on the trip to the airport, although in a distracted way, staring out the window of the Hummer. Hayley barely remembered the States—she hadn't been there since she was three, when Rachel and Hayley's father moved to Germany for his career in engineering. She could only remember Rachel's parents from their infrequent visits to Boblingen; she knew they were from Virginia, but didn't have a clue about their address or phone number. And with the Internet pooched the way it was, there was no way to track them online.

Rachel had listed Jax as her emergency contact on her hospice forms, which meant her parents didn't even know that she was gone yet. The idea of showing up at their door with that news and their virtual stranger of a granddaughter gave him a bellyache.

Rachel. He could feel despair pounding against the wall that years of training and counter-terrorism experience had built. Thoughts of her were the enemy right now: her raven hair, the way she stroked her dying patients' hands, the way she would cackle madly at Monty Python movies when Jax would simply stare at them and shake his head. The way she reminded him that the world wasn't just a desert full of people who wanted him dead.

Her dying words: *Take care of her. Promise me.*

"Next," the admin called from his seat behind the table.

Jax swallowed his emotion as he and Hayley stepped forward, hand in hand. The clerk spared them a blank look before returning his attention to his paperwork. Jax noticed with mild irritation that the man's black hair was considerably longer than military regulation.

"Name?"

"Capt. Jackson Booth, E-Company, 1st Battalion, 10th Special Forces Group." He gave him his Department of Defense ID number.

The man scribbled on his papers, then looked up at Hayley.

"Who's this?"

"I'm his guardian!" Hayley blurted, blood rushing into her cheeks.

Before Jax could say anything, the man looked back down at his papers, pen at the ready.

"Name?"

"Uh, Hayley," said Jax, confused. "Hayley Moore."

The man scribbled for a moment, then handed him two boarding passes with their names handwritten on them. He saw that Hayley's had been misspelled.

"Wait over there," the man said without looking up. "Next."

Jax shouldered his duffel and tugged Hayley along with him to the terminal's seating area to join his comrades. Something about the clerk's tone didn't sit right with him. Jax was Echo's commander—he didn't know for sure that he outranked the man, but he'd never met an army admin that wasn't a non-com, and definitely not one who dismissed a superior like that. At the very least, there should have been some sort of recognition. Ruben's words came back to him: *Shit's going sideways.*

Through the window walls he could see the tarmac virtually

covered in stationary airliners. It brought to mind sitting on the floor in the living room of the house he grew up in, watching the news coverage of the planes hitting the Twin Towers and seeing the airports with all the grounded jets. Jax had been too young to know what was going on, but he remembered his old man saying the sight of all those planes made him feel like the world had been turned upside down.

As they walked toward their gate, a woman in scrubs and a surgical mask approached and asked for their boarding passes. She gave each a cursory glance before ordering them to roll up a sleeve. Jax saw the fear in Hayley's eyes as the needle descended toward her shoulder.

"It's okay," he said quietly. "It won't hurt."

The girl didn't believe him and scrunched her face, but seemed none the worse for wear when it was over. A couple of chatting soldiers absently gave up their seats as the two approached, and Jax nodded his appreciation. Hayley sat down, still clutching her panda.

Jax looked at her little feet dangling above the floor and was hit with a sudden wave of something bordering on panic: who the hell was he to think he could take care of a child? Especially *this* one, who was the entire world to the woman he'd loved and now lost? There had to have been child services agencies in Stuttgart that could handle this. She could have gone to the consulate in Frankfurt. *Anything* that meant she didn't have to rely on him.

Is it really about her? he asked himself as he sat down beside her. *Or are you just scared?*

Before he could go any further down that path, Ruben appeared in front of them with a dark-haired woman in tow. Valentina Cruz had been a sergeant in Echo for a year, and was one of the first women accepted into active Special Forces combat duty after the ban was lifted a decade earlier. As always, her khaki T-shirt was straining against the enormous breasts and rippling muscles underneath it.

Jax nodded to the duo. He understood the plan immediately: Hayley would appreciate a female presence, and Val was pretty much it for the company.

"I'm Val," she said, kneeling in front of the girl's seat. "You're Hayley, right?"

Hayley nodded. Her eyes were wide as she looked over the woman's chiseled frame.

"I was going to go get a hot chocolate," Val said softly. "Sometimes hot chocolate helps me when I'm feeling rough. But I'm scared to go by myself—will you come with me?"

"You're not really scared," Hayley said with a tentative smile.

Val returned the smile and leaned in close. "You're right," she hissed in a stage whisper. "I just don't want to hang around all these smelly boys. So you wanna come?"

Hayley looked up at Jax, who nodded. Val took her hand and led her toward a coffee kiosk about fifty yards away.

"Thanks, man," he said as Ruben took the vacant seat next to him. "I don't know what the hell I'm doing. I can't look after a kid."

Ruben shrugged. "She's still alive. That's something."

"Very funny."

"The hot chocolate was Val's idea. I told her what happened and she said she wanted to help. She lost her own mom at a young age."

"So did I," said Jax. "That's not helping me with Hayley."

Ruben looked around the terminal and let out a long, slow breath.

"That's some 9-11 shit right there," he said, nodding at the windows.

"I was just thinking the same thing. My memories are pretty fuzzy from back then, but I distinctly remember my old man saying 'It ain't right to have that many birds on the ground'."

A bank of television screens over the seats opposite them showed a pair of local hosts on a Stuttgart morning show. English subtitles told a broken story of how there was only local news today because all of the wire services were down. The duo—a young blond woman and an older man with long black hair and odd square glasses—chatted as if this happened all the time, but Jax thought their smiles looked like the kind you'd see on the faces of people on a roller-coaster.

"I've never seen an airport this empty, either," said Ruben. "I mean, there isn't a single Chinese tourist anywhere."

"That's racist."

He flipped Jax the bird. "I'm serious. When was the last time you were in an airport here and you didn't see a group of passengers from China milling around?"

Ruben was right. Germany had become a mecca for Chinese immigrants and tourists alike after the Europeans signed the free trade deal back in 2022. It had been an economic boon for both nations and brought billions in investment to Europe. Jax had read that BMW had expanded its factory in Shenyang threefold to keep up with demand.

America hadn't fared so well. He and Ruben hadn't been stateside in six months, and things hadn't been looking too good back then. The economy was stumbling and the people seemed to be angry about everything, all the time. Jax wondered what was waiting for them when they got back home now.

"I don't think we're getting the full story on this virus," said Ruben, still staring out the window. "It's gotta have something to do with this Internet thing. I mean, look at the TV. Even the news people can't get online. I wouldn't be surprised if the whole damn country is down."

As if on cue, the screens above the seats went blank, then were replaced with a cartoon image of a man swearing at his television set. Jax's German wasn't great, but he knew what the words on the screen meant: *Technical difficulties, please stand by*.

"Great," he said. "Now you've gone and fucked up the TVs."

"This is serious. There's shit going on behind the scenes that we don't know about."

A sudden wave of exhaustion and frustration finally hit Jax, and his next words came out harsher than he'd intended.

"We're in the United States Army," he snapped. "There's always shit going on that we don't know about. It's not our job to question it; it's our job to follow orders."

Ruben looked like he had something more to say, but he kept his mouth shut. They were best friends, but Jax still had two silver bars on his shoulders to Ruben's single silver and black one, and arguing with the company commander was frowned upon in public places.

They were saved from awkward silence by Hayley and Cruz, who emerged from the concourse each carrying a deep blue Tchibo cup. Hayley still had her panda clutched in her other hand, but she looked marginally less catatonic than she had earlier, which Jax took as a win.

"Better?" he asked as the two joined them. Hayley nodded and sat down, but said nothing.

Cruz knelt over the girl and whispered in her ear. Hayley nodded and whispered something back. The sergeant locked eyes with Jax and tilted her head slightly as she stood up, a cue for him to follow her.

"I'll be right back," he said to Hayley. "Stay with Ruben."

Jax rendezvoused with Cruz near a charging station. "Thanks, Val, I appreciate that."

"Mind if I offer some unsolicited advice?" she asked, hands planted on her hips. Jax noted absently that her biceps were almost as big as his own.

"Go ahead," he said.

"That girl is broken, and you're treating her like some kind of burden. If you're not up to taking care of her the right way, you should pass her along to someone who can before you do any permanent damage." She caught herself after a beat and added, "Sir."

Jax ran a hand down his face, feeling the sandpaper on his cheeks. She wasn't telling him anything he didn't already know.

"That's good advice, Sergeant," he sighed. "And if you can find me anyone who can do that right now, I'll gladly take you up on it. But as far as I can see, there aren't even airport staff in this airport, let alone children's services. Until we can get her to her grandparents, she's my responsibility. I may be the last person she needs, but I'm the only one she's got."

He glanced over to see Ruben bent over in his seat, elbows on knees, talking to Hayley. She was responding instead of staring into the distance, at least.

"She's got me and the chief," said Cruz. "Remember that, all right?"

He nodded. "I will. Thanks."

She touched his arm briefly and left to join some other NCOs who were talking in a group near another seating area. That kind of behavior wouldn't fly in a lot of military situations, but Echo Company was unique. They spent too much time in the sights of terrorists to worry about the formalities of protocol. NCOs and officers might not have spent a lot of time together outside of work, but anyone who had your six in some dusty rat's nest in Mosul or a burnt-out apartment building in Damascus was family, regardless of rank.

"Booth!"

The sound of his name brought him out of his reverie. He looked across the concourse to see Col. Archer marching toward him, his bullet head gleaming in the noon sunlight that poured in through the windows. Twenty feet to his left, Ruben looked up at Archer and then at Jax before turning his attention back to Hayley.

"Sir," Jax replied. He inhaled deeply, let it out again. Time to face the music. "I can explain."

Archer frowned as he pulled up alongside him. His uniform looked somehow larger on him, as if he'd lost weight since Jax had last seen him. Between his own time with Rachel and the colonel's recent secondment to U.S. European Command here in Stuttgart, they hadn't been in the same room in weeks.

"Explain what?" Archer asked.

"The girl."

"What girl?" The colonel shook his head. "I don't care about a girl. We need to talk about what's waiting for us stateside."

Jax's spirits rose a tiny bit. Maybe, just maybe, he could pull this off and get Hayley where she needed to be.

"Sir." He nodded. "Awaiting orders."

"I don't need to tell you shit's gone sideways here," said Archer, unknowingly echoing Ruben. His eyes danced around the room, taking in everything around them. Jax had never seen the old guy so agitated.

"This situation gives a whole new meaning to FUBAR, Booth. I've seen more than my fair share of bullshit during forty years in this man's army, but Christ. Half of EUCOM is out sick with this fucking virus."

Jesus. *Half* of them? Jax was suddenly grateful for the little knot that had emerged in his arm where the needle had landed earlier.

"That's why it's just Echo Company on this mission," said Archer. "Top brass was asking for the only the best we've got, and you people are it. Besides, the Boblingen base's infirmary is starting to see its first virus cases from 1st Battalion members."

Jax's stomach dropped. "Is there any intel on where this thing came from, sir?" he asked.

"They're telling me North Korea, but who the hell knows? It's like children playing the old telephone game, where everyone adds their own little piece of bullshit until the message is unrecognizable. Especially now that communications are in the shitter. All I know is that we need to be ready for anything when we get into Colorado."

Jax nodded. "We always are, sir."

Archer gave him an appraising look, as if weighing whether he could trust his captain, then turned his gaze to the window walls looking out on the tarmac. The two had known each other for years; what was all this about? When the colonel finally spoke, the gravity in his voice was palpable.

"You've always been ready to face our enemies abroad," he said. "The ones who point guns at us and scream 'death to America!'"

Then he turned to face Jax, and his weathered face seemed to age even more, right before the younger man's eyes.

"Are you ready to stare down your fellow citizens on American soil, Jax?" His voice was gentler now. "People who are looking to you to save them from whatever the hell is going on? Are you ready to fire on them? Because, God help us, I think that's where this is headed."

Jax had only a moment to consider before a voice over the public address system told them it was time to board the plane to Atlanta.

3

If Stuttgart Airport had been chaos, Hartsfield-Jackson in Atlanta was bedlam. The moment Jax got to the jet bridge opening, Hayley in hand, he could hear commotion coming down from the terminal beyond. When they emerged into the airport, they were met with a swarm of people in white lab coats and surgical masks.

The eleven-hour flight had been a welcome reprieve from the crushing strangeness of the previous two days. Hayley, exhausted, had fallen asleep beside him in the window seat. Jax had followed suit, despite the constant chatter going on around them.

Archer and other mid-level brass had spoken in hushed tones in the business class seats at the front throughout the flight. Jax had noticed absently that the curt man who'd given him and Hayley their boarding passes was sitting in one of the dozen first-class seats as they entered the 747, but he forgot it almost instantly as they made their way to their seats in the rear.

Now, deplaning, Hayley clutched his hand tighter as Jax pushed his way through the sea of white. Ahead he could see a bank of unmanned customs kiosks, chained off and patrolled by armed men in what looked to be police riot gear, also wearing masks.

"It's okay," he told her, not believing his own words. "These are emergency people. They're here to help."

To his left, he saw Archer and a couple of the other brass he didn't recognize arguing with one of the whitecoats. The colonel's entire head seemed to be glowing red.

"I'm going to tell you this one more time," he growled. "Our orders are to continue on a United charter to Colorado Springs at 1630 hours. Anyone who gets in our way will be dealt with physically. Is that clear?"

The subject of his abuse, a woman with huge, owlish glasses and hair as white as her coat, shook her head.

"The Center for Disease Control has authority here," she said archly, her voice muffled by the cloth mask. "I told you, this is a quarantine zone."

Archer pinched the bridge of his hawk nose. "And *I* told *you* they've all been vaccinated."

"We don't have records in our database..."

"Of course you don't!" Archer snapped. "We only have handwritten papers here with us because the electronics in Stuttgart weren't working worth shit. So even if the electronics here in Atlanta are magically working just fine—which they're not—you're not going to see that information any time soon. And regardless of the situation, this company *will* be on that flight at 1630 hours. Is that clear?"

The woman blinked at him silently behind her comical glasses.

"All right then," Archer said.

He turned to face the crowd that had formed as the rest of the passengers were blocked by whitecoats. When he spoke, his voice made the woman in the glasses jump.

"Attention, Echo Company!" he barked. "We've got less than thirty minutes to hike about two miles to the domestic departures terminal and meet our connection, so start marching. If anyone gets in your way, you are to remove them. Anyone who is not at the gate at precisely 1630 hours will be left behind and court-martialed. Is that understood?"

"Yes, sir!" the crowd shouted in unison. Jax thought it felt good to finally do something familiar, if only for a few moments. Acknowledging orders, marching double-time—that was *normal.*

Hayley's eyes stared up at him under a furrowed brow. "Two miles? I can't—"

Before she could finish, Cruz appeared next to them and picked Hayley up by the waist, hoisting the startled girl over her head and onto her wide shoulders.

"No worries, soldier." Cruz turned to Jax. "We'll meet you at the gate, sir?"

He nodded, resisting the urge to sigh with relief. Fighting his instincts, he reached up and squeezed Hayley's hand. It's what Rachel would have wanted him to do.

"We'll get you to your grandparents," he said. "Me and the rest of Echo. You're one of us now."

She nodded and squeezed back. Cruz marched off through the crowd of whitecoats, shoving them aside as she passed. Dozens of others followed suit, eventually forming a moving wedge that pointed its way to the other side of the airport. Over by the customs kiosks, the men in riot gear looked nervous.

Ruben sidled up to Jax as he watched a handful of whitecoats join the woman with Archer and the other brass.

"This proves it, man," Ruben whispered. "This virus is way worse than they've been telling us."

"CDC's trying to take command of the situation," Jax whispered back. "Archer's telling them to piss up a rope. Come on, we need to get moving."

The two shouldered their packs and joined the others making their way through the whitecoats. As they passed Archer and crew, they noticed the man who'd checked them in back in Germany handing a satellite phone to the older woman from CDC.

"I know that, but..." Jax heard the woman say. There was a pause and then a terse: "Fine. Whatever." The last thing he could make out as they faded into the distance was: "...insanity... your funeral, not mine..."

"You see that dude sitting in first class on the way here?" Ruben asked, lifting his chin in the direction of the man Jax now suspected wasn't an ordinary admin.

Before he could answer, Jax heard Cruz raise her voice ahead of them.

"You heard the colonel!" she barked. "Move or be moved!"

Suddenly the troops in front of him started moving outwards in a circle; the space in between them opened up as they did, and Jax's stomach dropped as he caught sight of Cruz and Hayley facing three of the men in black who'd been stationed at customs. The men's AR-15 rifles were raised and pointed at the pair.

"The kid isn't in the army," said the man in front. "She's got no business going with you."

Instinct and training launched Jax forward, elbowing his way through the throng of soldiers who were surrounding their comrade in solidarity. He couldn't see any good outcome to this if he didn't de-escalate right fucking now.

"Stand down!" he ordered. Then he pointed at the three cops. "That goes for you, too! Stand down!"

"You're not in charge here!" countered the one in front, a stocky guy in his twenties with rivulets of sweat running down his wide face. His rifle was now pointed at Jax. "We're running shit, and I say the girl stays here."

His gut told him this kid had just been given a taste of power thanks to the shortage of able bodies, and he was enjoying it a little too much. Again, training told Jax to appear more in command than his opponent. He fixed his eyes on the man with a stare that would have drilled through concrete.

"Son, do you really want to piss off an entire company of elite Special Forces counter-terrorism specialists?" he growled. "Because that's what you're doing. Lower your weapons and let us pass. *Now!*"

He knew he was bluffing—none of Echo were armed—but he hoped the guy was intimidated enough that he wouldn't think about that.

He wasn't.

"I told you already, GI Joe," said the lead man in black, advancing until the barrel of his weapon was just inches from Jax's chest. Behind him, Jax heard Hayley gasp. "You're not in charge here."

Jax had been in enough situations in his career to know when fingers were about to squeeze triggers, and the look on the cop's face was enough to make him square his feet and prepare to reach for the barrel. He would try to pivot as he caught it, enough to either pull it from the cop's grip or a least immobilize the man's trigger finger, lessening the risk that he'd be shot.

Then a throb of adrenaline shot through his belly as he realized Hayley was directly behind him, in the line of fire.

Crack! Crack! Crack!

Three mini explosions filled his ears in the space of a quarter-second and he heard Hayley shriek behind him. Jax's training kicked in before his brain and he dove forward in a roll on the floor, emerging hunched over one knee, facing the direction the shots had come from. In his mind's eye, he saw Hayley lying in a pool of blood on the airport's gleaming tile floor.

Instead, he saw the man from first class levelling a nine-millimeter pistol at the men in riot gear. A thin wisp of smoke escaped the barrel.

Jax snapped his head in the direction of the cops just in time to see the three who had been threatening him slowly collapsing into heaps on the floor. Each of the three rounds had entered through the men's face guards, leaving them shattered and drenched in blood. Jax caught sight of the first man's face as he dropped—there was a crimson and black cave where his right eye had been. The hollow-point round had exploded on impact with the back of the man's skull, ripping a jagged hole in the Kevlar and plastic of his helmet as it exited. The other two's heads were in a similar state.

In his confusion, Jax noted that the man's shoulders had sprouted a pair of oak leaves at some point between Germany and Atlanta. He was a major, and hence the ranking officer between Jax and Archer right now.

The sounds of panic were spreading through the terminal as whitecoats bolted in all directions, but the members of Echo stood their ground. No one breathed as the shooter calmly approached the remaining three cops—at least, Jax assumed they were cops. They could have been civilians for all he knew.

He glanced up at Hayley to see that all the color had drained from her face. Still, a wave of relief washed through him. Thank God she was all right.

All right? She watches her mother die, now she sees three men murdered right in front of her, all in the space of two days? This is about as far from all right as you can get.

The major stopped ten feet from the rest of the men in riot gear, his non-regulation hair drooping down to his eyebrows. "If you want to live, get out of here," he said in a flat tone, like someone ordering from a drive-thru window. "Go find the people you care about and spend as much time with them as you can."

The nine-millimeter was still pointed in their direction. The men looked at each other, wide-eyed. Finally, one of them thumbed the safety into place on his rifle and tossed it to the floor.

"Fuck this," he breathed, pulling off his helmet. "Fuck *all* y'all!"

He tossed the helmet and took off down the concourse at a jog. Ten seconds later, his colleagues followed suit, leaving the soldiers unopposed in their journey to the other side of the airport.

By the time Jax had processed all this, the major had holstered his weapon and was walking toward Archer and the other brass as they marched in his direction. Jax thought the old man looked even more shaken now than he had back in Germany—not surprisingly—and his companions' faces shared a similar pale coloring. Whatever this was, it didn't originate with them.

The soldiers milled around for a few moments, staring at the bodies and muttering, before Archer shouted: *"You've got your orders! Sixteen-thirty hours! Double time!"*

Jax closed the gap between himself and Cruz. He briefly thought about taking Hayley's hand, but he doubted it would do her any good. Beside him, he saw the sergeant stroking the girl's calves as she held her in place on her shoulders. He couldn't begin to imagine what was going through Hayley's head right now; he was having a hard enough time processing it himself, and he was a highly experienced combat veteran.

A moment later and Ruben was at his side again.

"What'd I tell you?" his friend said quietly. "This is egregiously fucked up."

Jax wanted to tell himself to leave it to the people above him and just carry out his orders; this was beyond his pay grade. But he couldn't get Archer's words in Stuttgart out of his head: *Are you ready to point your weapons at your fellow citizens on American soil, Jax?*

The thought chilled him to his core. He *wasn't* prepared for it, and he doubted anyone else in Echo was, either. But they'd all just seen one man who was more than prepared to do just that. And that man had the support of their superior officers—or at least whoever was on the other end of that satellite phone had it. The result was the same.

Jax didn't need to be a company commander to know what the soldiers were thinking: who the fuck *was* this guy? And what was waiting for them in Colorado?

4

The 10th SFG was based at Fort Carson, less than ten miles from the Cheyenne Mountain Complex, so Jax had seen the edifice before. But now, with its face looming in the distance through the windshield of the army transport bus, he couldn't shake a particular word out of his mind. It was like a drowsy wasp at a late summer picnic that just wouldn't leave him alone.

The word was *fortress*.

The complex had been built into the eponymous mountain by the Army Corps of Engineers in the early 1960s to house the nerve center for the nascent North American Air Defense Command. It was essentially a hollowed-out bunker that had been filled with more than a dozen three-story buildings, along with an anthill of tunnels to house support systems. A self-contained electrical plant and life-support system, along with millions of gallons of fresh water courtesy of a natural spring, allowed it to keep as many as a thousand people alive at any given time, regardless of the circumstances outside the mountain.

The U.S. government had spent the equivalent of billions in today's dollars to ensure as many government types and generals as possible would survive a nuclear attack on American soil. Cheyenne was a monument to Cold War paranoia.

At least that's what Jax had thought up until a few days ago. Here, now, with Hayley snuggled next to him on the old vinyl bus seat, he wasn't so sure.

The checkpoint outside the entrance to the complex was a riot of soldiers milling around, looking at papers and gesturing frantically. Behind them, the mountain looked cheery and green in the bright sunshine, as if trying to distract from what was going on underneath it.

"Well, *that* inspires confidence," Ruben drawled from the seat behind him as the bus rolled up to the security gate. "Classic clusterf—" He suddenly remembered Hayley and didn't finish.

"Archer's already here," said Jax. "We're pre-cleared. I couldn't get much out of him, but based on what he did tell me, I think Echo is here for a specific reason. The rest of the 1st Battalion is still in Germany. The other four battalions are up the road at Fort Carson, but none of the members are here."

"Huh. Why you think they need counterterrorism specialists to deal with a pandemic?"

"Ours is not to reason why."

Ruben glowered. "Ours is but to sit around and wonder what the fff...heck is going on."

Jax saw Ruben glance down at Hayley as she stared silently at the commotion outside the bus. He doubted she would have heard the word even if Ruben had finished it. She was starting to look as bedraggled as the panda she hadn't let out of her clutches since they left the hotel in Boblingen.

"Don't worry," he told her. "We'll find people here who can contact your grandparents."

She hadn't spoken much since the incident in Atlanta, and had slept—or at least pretended to—for the entire flight to Colorado Springs. No one had been particularly talkative on the plane; Archer's sidestepping of the incident at the airport had been as clear as if he'd given an order. *Pay no attention to the dead men on the floor. Get your asses on that fucking plane.*

Are you ready to fire on them? Archer had asked. *Because, God help us, I think that's where this is headed.*

Hayley's exhaustion was obvious, and Jax's heart cramped at the thought of how much she'd already suffered, and of what very likely was still ahead of them before he could get her to Rachel's parents. Cruz and the rest of Echo had gone out of their way to be kind to her, but she wasn't some mascot for a company of battle-hardened soldiers. She was a sweet, innocent kid—at least she had been until she met him.

He was prepared to get off the bus and show the guards the company's orders, but they simply opened the big iron gate and waved them through. The crowd of soldiers parted to make way for them, then reformed behind them as the bus rolled slowly toward the entrance to Cheyenne Mountain Complex. For the first time ever, the sight of the hole in the mountain made Jax think of the mouth of a giant monster.

"OKEY DOKEY," said the compact redheaded corporal behind the stack of electronic components. "Jenny and Richard Townshend, where are you?"

Her name was Brown and she appeared to be all of twenty years old. Around her, the small room was chock-a-block with wires and boxes. It was one of a half-dozen communications centers that had been set up at Cheyenne in an attempt to either work around whatever computer virus had been hobbling electronics across the U.S. for the past few weeks, or to leapfrog over it with technology that didn't need to follow established Internet channels for comms.

Jax watched the woman's eyes flit across the three screens in front of her. He couldn't begin to make sense of the stacks of dusty old radio equipment that had obviously been hauled out of a storage closet. It seemed like she was somehow working the two technologies together, which he supposed wasn't all that strange: on a fundamental level, wi-fi relied on radio waves. That was about the depth of his understanding, though.

Beside him, Hayley gripped his hand with a strength he wouldn't have thought possible from a ten-year-old.

"O-kayyy," Brown muttered, more to herself than them, as her fingers tap-danced on the keyboard. "That's not you... uh-uh... nope..."

"Are you getting a lot of demands on your time?" Jax asked, hoping to break some of the tension. Searching could take some time, and he wasn't sure his hand was up to the punishment from Hayley's grip.

"Yes, sir," she said. Her eyes never left the screen. "Even when people can get onto the Internet, there are thousands of sites down. All social media, Amazon, YouTube. Every dot-gov site comes up blank."

"Guess we have to resort to actually talking to each other on the phone," he said with a half-hearted smile.

"Cell coverage is pretty spotty, too. And when people *can* get through, a lot of them are saying that no one is answering. Even texts."

Jax rubbed his unshaven cheeks. He'd been hearing similar stories from the members of Echo Company. He himself didn't have anyone to get in touch with; his parents were long gone and he'd been an only child. Special Forces was his family. Rachel's had been the sole civilian number in the contact list of his cheap Chinese smartphone.

Darkness was the order of the day, it seemed. Ever since they'd arrived at Cheyenne, Echo had been relegated to getting stowed away in their new quarters in the sprawling complex. Jax hadn't heard from Archer at all, which rankled him. He'd never seen such a breakdown in the chain of command in all his years in the army. Orders kept the machine moving; when you didn't have them, it was too easy for the machine to seize up, which made it that much harder to get moving again when you needed it.

At least Hayley had perked up a little bit at the sheer novelty of the complex. Buildings inside of a mountain never failed to impress visitors to Cheyenne, and she was no exception. They had been allowed to wander some of the corridors to get oriented, but while she took it all in, the knot in Jax's gut had continued to grow. There should have been more people there. It was built to hold upwards of a thousand, but he estimated he'd seen less than half of that, and sixty-eight of those had been Echo Company.

"I think I may have something, sir," the young woman said, pulling Jax out of his thoughts. She turned the right-hand screen toward them so they could see it. On it was a photo of a middle-aged couple seated side-by-side on a hay wagon. The woman's eyes looked so much like Rachel's that Jax felt a stab in his heart.

"That's them!" Hayley cried, letting go of his hand. "I remember! That's them!"

"I managed to get into a Facebook archive that was hosted off the main site."

"Can you get to the profile page?" Jax asked.

Brown scrunched her freckled face. "I can try, but I'm betting they don't have a phone number listed. The best I can do is to send an email to the address on the account."

Hayley's face dropped. Jax knelt beside her and looked her in the eye.

"It's something," he said. "We'll just have to wait a bit for them to answer. When they do, we'll get their number and we'll call as soon as we can. Okay?"

She fixed him with a look that was becoming far too common on her young face: bitter disappointment. Each time he saw it, it crushed him a tiny bit more.

"Okay," she whispered.

"I'll get in touch the second I hear back from them," Brown said with a sympathetic smile.

"Thank you," said Jax. Hayley was already out the door and headed back into the hall.

"I wish I had had more," the corporal said, then leaned in closer and lowered her voice. "To be honest, sir, we haven't been getting a lot of responses from outside of El Paso County for the last twenty-four hours. Even on official military channels."

He frowned. "The computer virus is getting worse, then?"

"I don't think it *is* a virus," she said. "The more we see of it, the more it looks like it was a weaponized code of some sort. But even the analog channels are quiet. This base has the most secure military communications system in the Western Hemisphere, even without the Internet. The messages are getting through—people just aren't picking up."

Jax tried not to think about the implications of that as he nodded his thanks and joined Hayley in the hallway.

DEEP in the heart of a mountain, it was impossible to tell that night had fallen as Jax put Hayley to bed in the bunk above Cruz. As the only female member of Echo Company, she'd never had a problem bunking with men, but she requested to be housed in the group of rooms that had been designated as the women's barracks for Hayley's sake.

Jax had noticed a distinct lack of female personnel at Cheyenne—surely no more than thirty—which reinforced his suspicion that the upper brass was stacking the deck with experienced combat troops.

A couple of off-duty Air Force airmen—he still shook his head at calling women "men"—offered to keep Hayley company for the night after hearing her story from Cruz. By the time he had settled things with them, the girl was snoring softly in her cot, her battered panda tucked tightly under her chin.

As he made his way down to the mess hall that had been assigned to Echo, he could already feel Cheyenne's sterile hallways closing in on him. How people managed to live here year-round was beyond him—it hadn't even been two full days and Jax felt like he was bottled up in a submarine.

The mess itself was another featureless building lined with long tables next to an open kitchen. It reminded Jax of the American Legion hall in his hometown back in Texas, except instead of the Ladies' Auxiliary doing the cooking, it was soldiers on KP.

Ruben caught sight of Jax and waved him over to a table. He was sitting with two other men—Jax could tell by the slight variations in their fatigues that one was an airman and the other a marine—and eating from a silver mess tray. Jax filled his own tray and joined them.

"Gentlemen," he said as he took a seat next to the airman. "Don't get up. What am I about to eat?"

Ruben wrinkled his nose. "Well, if I was going on looks alone, I'd say pig vomit. But I think it's spaghetti and some kind of bean soup." He motioned to the two men. "Speaking of pig vomit, this marine here is Gunnery Sergeant Lee."

Lee, a muscular Asian with a narrow face and a bare skull, saluted and nodded. "Captain."

"Sergeant," Jax replied, returning the salute. "Pig vomit is not official army policy regarding marines, just so you know."

"That's a relief, sir," he said somberly.

"Long way from home, aren't you? Closest marine base is Yuma."

"Yessir. Special assignment. Commercial flight from Bridgeport two days ago."

Jax chewed that over—why did Bridgeport ring a bell? Before anything could register, Ruben nodded to the airman next to Jax, a wiry gent in his forties with salt-and-pepper hair. "This is Chief Master Sergeant Campbell."

Another exchange of salutes.

"More reconstituted food," Jax mused. It was all they'd been served since they got here. "Better than MREs, I suppose, but not a hell of a lot."

"We've been on MREs at Schriever for the past week," said Campbell. "I'll take this any day."

That surprised Jax. Meals Ready to Eat were combat rations—why would an air force base like Schriever be on rations? But it wasn't his place to question another branch, so he kept it to himself.

"So," said Ruben, "Special Forces, with a few marine specialists, some army and air force support, all tucked into the world's biggest bomb shelter. Eating food that only requires water and heat in a place that has an endless supply of both. Nothing to see here, right?"

Jax sighed. "Did you join the army so you could be a smartass, Chief? Because if you did, you're on the fast track to promotion. I'll make sure to pass along my recommendation to Col. Archer."

"I'm just saying what everyone's thinking," he said. "Sir."

Ruben's familiarity around outsiders bothered Jax a bit, but not enough that he let it show. These were extraordinary circumstances, to say the least. Still, at a time when the chain of command seemed to be missing a few links, he wondered if it might not be best to tighten instead of loosen.

"So you both just got here, too?" he asked.

They nodded. Lee said: "I'm just happy to be away from Bridgeport. Whatever this virus is, it hit there hard; the airfield was practically deserted when I flew out. I mean, yeah, I was vaccinated, but shit. That's an ugly disease."

"Sounds an awful lot like what we saw in Atlanta," said Ruben. Jax could hear the smugness in his voice. "And Stuttgart, for that matter."

"Same with the Springs," said Campbell. "Guys were dropping like flies at Schriever right before I left. The infirmary was busting at the seams because there weren't any beds at the hospitals in the city."

As he tucked into his food, Jax glanced at the third finger of each man's left hand. Neither of them were married. He'd done a head count of Echo Company in Stuttgart before he left, and the four men who hadn't shown up at the airport were the four members who had families in Germany. Everyone who was here in Cheyenne was single.

That might mean nothing, he told himself. Or it might mean something. If command expected things to get ugly, it would make sense for them to send in men with less to lose.

Or maybe this place was making him paranoid.

"Any idea when orders will be coming down, sir?" Campbell asked. "All we were told is that Col. Archer is in charge until further notice."

Jax shook his head. "Tomorrow, maybe. Archer's been surrounded by brass since we got here; he's probably still wrapping his head around things, same as us."

Lee chimed in. "I'm betting some of the work will be hauling away all those abandoned vehicles on the roads. Must've been a hundred of 'em on the way here from the airport."

Jax had seen them. He wondered what the hell went through people's heads; you think you can drive away from a virus? And from what he'd seen since they got back stateside, gas was as precious as gold these days. He didn't know what their orders would be, but he was sure it would go far beyond just towing vehicles from the side of the road.

Ruben's eyes flicked above Jax's head; he turned around on the bench to face the large video screen that had been set high up on the wall behind him and saw the haggard face of their commander-in-chief. Much like Archer, Terrence Fletcher seemed to have aged years since the last time Jax had seen him, and it made his guts twist. He wasn't Fletcher's biggest fan, but he respected the office. It was obviously weighing heavy on the man.

The signal was far from clear; Fletcher's head kept breaking into blocks of black pixels and then reforming. Somewhere out of sight, someone hit the volume button.

"Finally," said Ruben. "Maybe we'll get some answers here."

"That's Air Force One," Campbell said, eyes narrowed. "He's on his way here from Edwards, I bet."

Jax held up a hand to silence them. "My fellow Americans," the president said in scratchy audio that wasn't fully synched with the video. "It is with the heaviest of hearts that I address you this evening..."

No one spoke for a long time after the broken signal ended. There were large chunks that had been lost in the transmission process, but the message of the president's speech was clear: America was under martial law, and the National Guard was mobilizing.

Jax noticed Lee and Campbell looking at him expectantly, clearly waiting for something from the senior officer in the room. What the hell was he supposed to say? He'd been sitting beside them when the president made the direst proclamation in the nation's history. He didn't have any clearer view of the future than they did.

"Jesus," Ruben breathed. "National Guard rule. Never thought I'd see the day."

"That doesn't explain what we're doing here," said Campbell. "We can't do much for the Guard from Cheyenne. And what about the rest of the Forces?"

"I'm a marine," said Lee. "The Guard is army and air force. What am *I* doing here?"

"Maybe that's what Archer and the rest are here to figure out," said Jax. "There's never been a domestic response like this before; I imagine there are massive logistics to be figured out."

"And Echo is here for logistics?" Ruben asked. "We're counter-terrorism specialists."

Jax's frustration finally broke through his veneer. *"I don't fucking know!"* he barked. "Is that what you all want to hear? Fine, there it is. *I don't fucking know.*"

The three men avoided his gaze as the ones in the kitchen hurried to look busy. Jax felt ashamed at losing it like that, but the stress of the last three days was starting to eat through his soul—and the lining of his stomach, judging by the growling pain that had been building there.

"Look, I—" he began before he was cut off by the squawk of the radio on his hip. They'd been using walkies since they got here, since they weren't able to rely on cell service.

"Booth!" It was Archer's voice.

Finally, Jax thought as he unclipped it from his belt and held it to his mouth.

"Booth here, sir. Awaiting orders, over."

"Command center. *Now.*"

"Yessir."

He replaced the radio on his hip and leapt from his seat. As he strode toward the exit to the mess, he glanced back at the men.

"Looks like orders are on their way, gentlemen," he said. "Be careful what you wish for."

5

Marcus Chase looked at his fingernails in the glare light of the fluorescents that ran the length of the ceiling in the room that now served as a makeshift stockade. Ever since he was a young teen, they'd covered little more than two-thirds of the skin at the tips of his tapered fingers. He was a chewer, making a regular meal of the ragged strips of dead cells whenever they got more than an eighth of an inch past the quick.

Now, though, they were long. Practically luxuriant, compared to what they'd been for the past fifty-some years. For a brief moment, he wondered what they'd look like painted and buffed. Then he chuckled and shook his head.

His entire life he'd been a worrier, constantly running through every possible scenario in his head, feeling every possible outcome. In addition to ragged nails, the trait had resulted in one of the most distinguished careers of any military man in American history. He'd retired a full general before being named Secretary of Defense by Terrence Fletcher some seven years earlier, to acclaim from both sides of Congress.

These days, though, he no longer questioned himself. Maybe it was the death sentence he was living under; maybe it was just that he was sure that what he was doing was the right thing. Whatever the case, his nails had finally grown out.

"You wouldn't happen to have a Tylenol, would you?" he said softly to the soldier who stood ten feet away, a hand propped on his holstered weapon and a nervous look in his face. "You did a number on my skull when you brought me in here. Nice job, by the way."

The soldier glanced up at a closed circuit camera mounted over the locked door of the makeshift cell.

"I told you, son," said Chase. "It doesn't work. Outside of the radios, there's not much comms tech here that *does* work anymore. Sit down, if you want; we probably have a good ten minutes until he shows up."

The soldier looked confused and stood his ground.

"Suit yourself," Chase said with a shrug. "Private Peterson, right?"

The younger man nodded uncertainly.

"I know we don't really know each other, but it just seems weird for us to sit here and not talk, given the—I don't know, *personal* nature of what's about to happen."

Peterson blinked several times before finally walking over to the table where Chase sat with his hands cuffed in front of him. He didn't sit, but he did stand at ease.

"That's better," said Chase. "You were making me nervous."

A chuckle escaped the soldier before he clamped down on it.

"Go ahead and laugh," said the older man. "Might as well. The Secretary of Defense is sitting here facing a treason charge for sending drones to shoot down the President of the United States. I can't imagine anything more ridiculous, myself."

Peterson cleared his throat and Chase noticed a patina of sweat on the soldier's upper lip.

"How're your symptoms, son?"

"Not bad yet."

"They get a lot worse a lot quicker than you expect," he sighed. "But at least you won't suffer through that. And you know your wife and kids are vaccinated. That's about all anybody can hope for, given what's to come in the days ahead."

"Yessir." Peterson's gaze was far away.

"I'm curious: how much did they tell you? About the situation, I mean? About why we're doing this?"

The soldier shrugged. "Enough, I guess."

"And do you agree with the reasoning? Or did you just go along for your family's sake?"

Peterson shrugged again. "For what it's worth, I don't think you're wrong, sir."

Chase nodded. "You want to hear something stupid?"

"What's that?"

"Believe it or not, I'm naturally immune. Last blood test, I still didn't have any signs of Eko. One of the first exposed, ground zero when the North Koreans let it loose, and still nothing. Almost everyone else who was with me in those days is already dead. Well, there's one other whose fate I don't know, but I'm pretty sure he's gone by now, too."

Peterson's eyes narrowed. "That's crazy."

Chase let out a papery laugh.

"It's a real motherfucker of a joke, isn't it?" he said quietly. "Everyone's dropping from the virus, and the one guy who isn't has an inoperable, golf-ball-sized tumor pressing down on his cerebellum." He chuckled again. "At least I don't have to worry about it punching my ticket."

The soldier looked him in the eye. Chase nodded.

"On that note," he said. "I suppose it's time, isn't it?"

"Yessir."

"All right, then."

Chase stood—he was a good six inches taller than his guard—and held out his cuffed wrists. Peterson took a key from his belt and unlocked one cuff. Then he took his sidearm from its holster and handed it to the older man.

"It'll be quick," said Chase. "I promise."

Peterson nodded, his eyes on the wall. "Yessir."

Chase positioned himself behind the guard and draped his left arm across his chest. His right hand hefted the sidearm, a coppery-gray SIG Sauer.

"Nice weapon, the SIG. I was always a Beretta man myself."

Before Peterson could answer, the knob on the door to the makeshift stockade started to turn. Chase clamped his forearm around the soldier's throat and pressed his lips against his ear.

"Showtime, son," he hissed. "Remember: your country owes you a debt of gratitude."

6

Jax tried to hurry down the corridors without looking like he was hurrying, which wasn't easy.

Archer had ordered him not to draw attention to himself as he made his way to the room where the Secretary of Defense, Gen. Marcus Chase himself, was being held under guard on charges of treason after readily admitting to using two experimental drones to shoot down Air Force One with all aboard. Jax was going to begin preliminary interrogation to find out why.

His own words came back to haunt him: *Be careful what you wish for.*

He was still reeling from Archer's revelation that President Fletcher had been killed just minutes after the broadcast from AF1 had ended. The colonel had looked on the verge of a nervous breakdown as he passed along the news. Around them, generals and other colonels from both the army and the air force milled about the command center, reading printouts and looking at screens.

Orders had come down directly from Chairman of the Joint Chiefs, Marine Gen. Geoff Benton: get answers out of Chase at all costs.

"I want you in that room with him," Archer had told him quietly.

"I told these people that no one would have a better chance of getting answers from Chase than you. You're discreet and you're good at—well, at getting answers fast."

Jax was both of those—after so many years interrogating terrorists, he had to be—but at the moment, he felt like a blindfolded baby crawling around the rim of a shark tank.

"Chase has to be out of his head," he said. "The man has a Medal of Honor. He *campaigned* for Fletcher, for Christ's sake."

Archer nodded, frowning. "And yet he walked right into this room and told everyone he'd just shot down Air Force One. He put his hands out to be cuffed. His guard detail said he went peacefully, even though one of them gave him a cuff to the head on the way to his room."

Jax shook his head. "Could it—I mean, is it possible that it's... Eko?" The thought made his stomach turn. The situation they were facing was impossible enough without the fear that Eko victims were going to start losing their minds.

"That's just it," said Archer. "He's clean. No sign of infection at all. There's scuttlebutt about a possible brain tumor, but if he had one, he would have been bound to report it to the president. That's why we need answers. Are you up to the interrogation?"

Jax ran a hand through his hair and blew out a breath. "Yes, sir," he said quietly. "But first... I may be overstepping my boundaries here, but I have to ask: what the hell is going on here at Cheyenne?"

Archer scanned the room. "We're making ad hoc decisions together until Colton Raines gets here."

"The vice-president is coming *here?*" Jax's eyes widened.

"He's likely the president by now. Emergency swearing in on board Air Force Two right after it left Washington."

"But why Cheyenne?" He caught himself. "That's above my pay grade, sir. I apologize."

Archer leaned in and lowered his voice even more. "It's a fair question, but you're not going to like the answer. The consensus in this room is that the National Guard scheme is just palliative."

"Palliative?"

"The members weren't vaccinated, and now there's no X-57 left. No means of making any more. Once the CBRN suits run out, the Guard will start to die alongside the general public. We haven't been getting the full story on Eko. The mortality rate is far higher than we first believed. Those fucking Koreans opened Pandora's box, Booth, and we're left to deal with it."

Jax tried to grasp what it all meant, but his brain wouldn't allow him to make the leap. Surely it wasn't as bad as all that. The world still made sense—didn't it?

The defense secretary just killed the president. How much sense does that make?

"What are you saying, sir?"

Archer was whispering now. "I'm saying that I believe Echo Company was brought here to protect this base from whatever might be left when this country is done tearing itself apart. Once Raines gets here, Cheyenne Mountain is going to be the seat of government for the foreseeable future, God help us all."

THE YOUNG CORPORAL stationed outside the stockade room saluted as Jax approached. He returned it and dismissed the soldier.

"Sir?"

"Orders from Col. Archer. Keeping ears to a minimum."

The corporal looked a bit confused but nodded his understanding and strode off down the corridor. Jax couldn't blame the kid; he was guarding the door of a prisoner whom many of the people in this base had considered a personal hero. Jax supposed they still did, since news of what he'd done wasn't general knowledge yet. They would know soon, though not in the way Jax expected.

He had idolized Marcus Chase as a young man himself. The guy's story was a Hollywood screenwriter's wet dream: grew up on the mean streets of Baltimore, discovered ROTC at community college, which got him a 2nd lieutenant commission when he signed up in the army. Over four decades, he'd worked his way up to command roles, then strategic ones, and finally to politics, first as national security advisor, then as SecDef. He'd earned points among the public and the pundits for offering the civilian president a guiding hand through the foreign policy minefield that had emerged after the U.S. economy took its long nosedive.

And then he'd murdered the man. The President of the United States. His friend. Because apparently the world just wasn't quite fucked up enough as it was, with the Eko virus and whatever the hell was going on with computers. Shit was well and truly going sideways.

Jax took a deep breath and turned the knob of the featureless white door. It opened to reveal the last thing he would have expected: Chase was holding a service pistol to his guard's right temple.

Adrenaline slammed through Jax's system as his right hand went reflexively to his own sidearm and his left went up in a calming gesture.

"Mr. Secretary," he heard himself say. "You don't want to do that."

Chase fixed him with a wide stare as his grip tightened around the guard's throat. "You don't see them," he hissed. "They're here. Don't spook them."

"It's my fault," the guard gurgled. "He said he had to pee..."

"SHUT UP!" Chase bellowed, digging the SIG's barrel into the guard's temple. His voice dropped to a whisper again. "They'll *see* us."

Jax's heart jackhammered in his chest. He'd faced plenty of insane circumstances in combat, but never something like this. He was an interrogator, not a negotiator. He took a tentative step into the room.

"Don't," Chase said in a warning tone. "Just don't. Friendly isn't coming. The juice is loose."

"No, sir," Jax said, desperate to keep the conversation going. "Friendly isn't coming. But we're going to be okay. It'll all be okay if you just put the gun down."

The guard choked a cough as Chase pulled him farther into the room.

"He's... lost it," the guard croaked. "FUBAR..."

The SecDef's eyes danced wildly, then stopped to bore into Jax's.

"The times, they are a-changing..." he said as he let go his grip on the guard. The younger man stumbled to his left as Chase's arm straightened out and placed the SIG's barrel against the guard's temple again.

Jax let battle-hardened instinct take over, allowing his right hand to pull the sidearm from his holster and aim it at Chase's sternum.

"Mr. Secretary..."

"Noises off," Chase said and squeezed the trigger. The explosion pressed against Jax's eardrums as the slug exited the guard's skull, painting the white wall in brain matter and bone fragments.

"JESUS!" Jax heard someone shout before registering that it was his own voice. His hand reflexively gripped his own weapon as Chase turned the gun toward him.

"It's coming," the old man said sadly, leveling the weapon at Jax's head.

Jax's finger squeezed the trigger four times. Two slugs struck home in the upper lobes of Chase's lungs, knocking him back several steps. A third tore open his throat while the final one vaporized a large portion of his jaw. His narrow frame dangled there for a moment like a marionette before finally dropping to a heap on the floor.

Jax slowly closed the ten-yard gap between them, pistol still trained on the old man, heart still galloping in his chest. No motion from either of the downed men. They were dead as dead could be.

It took another thirty seconds for the outer guard he'd dismissed to return with others. By the time they burst through the door, Jax had placed his weapon on the table at the front of the room and was kneeling with his hands clasped behind his head.

"It's not what it looks like," he said. "I need to talk to Col. Archer."

As the guard yanked his hands behind his back and clicked the cuffs into place, Jax's thoughts weren't on explaining his story. They were on Chase's last words: *It's coming.*

7

"Get those off of him!" Archer barked as he stormed into the office that was serving as Jax's own stockade. "He's not under arrest."

The guard jumped at the order and unlocked the cuffs, then hurried out after Archer told him to leave him and Jax alone in the room.

Jax rubbed his wrists and nodded to his CO as he stood. "Thank you, sir. I'm sorry it went down the way it did."

"Christ, man," said Archer. "If I'd had any idea what you were walking into—"

He shook his head. "It was a FUBAR situation, sir. Nothing anyone could have done. I just wish I would have seen what was coming."

Archer shook his head. "If Chase hadn't shot that private, I fucking would have, for gross incompetence. He should have let Chase piss himself before he let him out of his restraints."

"Chase was incoherent the whole time I was with him. I'm no medic, but if he wasn't hallucinating, I'll eat my green beret."

Archer looked pensive. "Drugs? It doesn't make any sense. But then what *does* make any fucking sense these days?"

"Is it possible he just snapped?"

"Anything's possible," the old man sighed. "But I'd rather have a better story for the masses. Marcus Chase's epitaph shouldn't be 'went crazy, killed the POTUS'."

"Yessir. I'll follow whatever the official story ends up being."

"I appreciate that, son. Like it or not, truth is usually the first casualty of war."

Jax frowned. "Are we at war, sir?"

"I don't know what else to call it. All I know is that you and your men will have plenty to do, and soon."

"Yessir."

"I need to keep you with me until we have the story straight. I'm sure there are already a dozen rumors going around about those five gunshots, so we have to make sure we're all on the same page."

JAX'S WATCH told him he'd been in the breakout room off the main command center for less than two hours, but his aching muscles suggested it had been more like a year. He wished he was the type who could nap, but he wasn't; he was either fully asleep or fully awake. Being the latter, his mind refused to stop working even as he leaned back in the deep leather of the office chair, fingers laced behind his head.

Cheyenne was starting to feel like a prison. With no windows to the outside, and with an information blackout inside, they might as well be in some undersea cave. He remembered a poster that used to hang on the wall of the poker room that his father had fashioned out of the old tool shed beside the barn: it was a cartoon toadstool and said *I must be a mushroom—everyone keeps me in the dark and feeds me bullshit.*

On that note, he hoped that Hayley's bunk was far enough from the incident that she hadn't heard the shots fired and was still asleep. If it wasn't, he hoped Cruz or one of the airmen-women had enough sense to tell her it was just target practice.

The digital clock on the wall read 0211 when the door finally opened. Jax expected to see Archer, but he didn't expect the tall drink of water who walked in beside him: Colton Raines, former army ranger and fellow Texan, and one of Jax's personal heroes.

And, as of a few hours ago, the newly-minted President of the United States.

Jax lurched awkwardly to his feet and threw up a salute that bounced painfully off his forehead.

"At ease, Captain," Raines chuckled, returning the salute.

"Capt. Jackson Booth," Archer said by way of introduction as he closed the door behind him. "I think you know who this is."

"It's an honor, sir."

Raines looked like he'd been dragged through a knothole backwards, as Jax's father had been fond of saying. His shirt was rumpled and the tie was long gone; the sleeves had been rolled up high and showed off his ropy forearms. At sixty, he was a decade older than the man he'd replaced, and probably more respected by people on both sides of the political fence—assuming politics even existed anymore. But there was no mistaking the toll the past forty-eight hours had taken on the man.

"The honor's mine," Raines said, motioning his companions to sit. A lone man in a black suit stood next to the door with his hands clasped in front of him, staring blankly ahead. Jax wondered absently if the corded earpiece hanging from the man's ear even worked anymore.

"The president wanted to debrief you as soon as he heard what went down," said Archer.

"Let's get one thing clear right from the get-go," said the president. "You did what you had to do, Captain."

"Sir." Jax nodded.

"Col. Archer told me that the secretary was talking crazy at the end. Rest assured, he wasn't on drugs. At least, not that I know of." He sighed heavily. "Marcus had brain cancer."

Jax let that sink in. He wasn't sure if knowing that made him feel better or worse about what he'd been forced to do.

"President Fletcher was aware of it, and allowed him to continue with his duties," Raines continued. "I guess hindsight is 20/20. It's a safe bet that the stress of our...*current situation* was a contributing factor to his behavior. Did he show any signs of recognition when you were facing him?"

"No, sir," Jax said. "He was highly agitated. When he pulled the trigger on Peterson, I don't think he even realized what he'd done."

It's coming.

Raines sighed. "All right, I think we're all on the same page. We tell the American public that a great man was laid low by an illness through no fault of his own. Marcus Chase was a tragic figure, not a monster."

"Sir, if I may," said Archer. "We do have another possible narrative."

Raines raised his palms for him to continue. Archer glanced at the Secret Service agent, then back at Raines, who nodded.

"It was an enemy attack," said Archer. "The Chinese sent those drones. Their agent, Private Peterson, then shot the secretary, and Booth here killed Peterson before he could finish his murder spree." He motioned to the door. "Chase never came into the command center and surrendered. He remains a hero, and we have a visible enemy."

Raines leaned back in his chair and tented his fingers under his chin, but said nothing. Jax watched it unfold with rapt attention. He was used to battlefield chaos, not political maneuvering.

Archer continued, "We go public with our intel that Eko is a weaponized virus. We know it's a coordinated attack by North Korea, and for all we know, China was behind it. In fact, more and more evidence is tracing whatever the hell is fucking with our computers back to them as well."

The colonel glanced at Jax, then back to the president.

"Permission to declassify?"

Raines nodded. "After everything he's been through, I'd say it's the least we can do."

Jax perked up. Finally, some questions would be answered.

Archer looked him in the eye. "Things are bad, son. I'm sure you've already started to suspect."

"That incident in Atlanta was a hint," he said, hoping it didn't come across as sarcasm.

"It was." Archer nodded. "We don't have the luxury of fucking around anymore. Eko's death rate here in the continental U.S. is over 98 percent, with a rate of infection around the same. Less than four percent were vaccinated before the X-57 ran out, and the majority of those were military personnel."

For a full five seconds, Jax forgot to breathe. Ninety-eight percent? He couldn't wrap his head around the figure. There were 340 million people in the U.S. That meant that almost 333 million people would contract Eko, and of those, some 326 million would die. Or already *had* died.

Archer scowled. "I did the math in my head when I got the figures, too," he said. "It's hard to comprehend. We're looking at a post-Eko population of under 15 million in the entire United States. For comparison, that's about what it was in the 1830s."

Raines ran a big hand through his silver hair. His face looked heavy in the odd light of the breakout room, like a statue's.

"It's enough to make you want to just run off into the night and not look back," he said quietly. "But there's nowhere to run to. All of our intel—hell, common sense alone—tells us the rest of the world isn't faring any better."

Jax let out out a shaky breath. "And this was all a *weapon?*"

Archer nodded. "All this time we were worried about those crazy bastards developing ICBMs. Turns out we should have been more concerned about them fucking sneezing on us."

"They couldn't have thought they could contain something like that..."

"This is Kim Jong Un we're talking about," said Raines. "The one relationship even Terry Fletcher couldn't figure out. Once China cut all ties with North Korea, things went even further off the rails than they already had been. Intel reports say there was a massive famine that made the 1990s look tame by comparison. We were too busy with insurgencies and terrorism in the Middle East to pay much attention to the peninsula." He gave Jax a wan smile. "Look who I'm talking to about the Middle East. You've been in the heart of it."

"Yessir. No disrespect, but I wish I was back there right now. I'd take insurgents over this any day."

Raines snorted a rueful laugh. "I'd be right beside you, soldier."

"You can see where this is headed," said Archer. "For better or worse, Cheyenne Mountain is the most secure place we have to ride out the crisis. That's why President Fletcher was on his way here, and it's why President Raines is here now. And it's why Gen. Benton ordered Echo Company here."

Jax nodded. "You need soldiers who are ready for anything."

"And who are ready to *do* anything," said Archer. "You remember our talk in Stuttgart?"

Jax got his meaning and it turned his stomach. He nodded, picking up the hint that Archer didn't want to talk about it in front of the president. Not that it would have come as a shock to the man. He doubted anything would shock anyone in the room at this point.

"First things first," said Raines. "We have to decide on the narrative for Chase. I'm going to leave it up to you, Captain. I agree that there are distinct advantages to the colonel's suggestion, but I'm not going to order you to lie. I refuse to make that my first act as commander-in-chief."

Raines had a reputation as a straight shooter, and for the moment Jax allowed himself to be glad his fellow Texan would be at the helm during this crisis. He would never have wished ill on Terrence Fletcher, but he wasn't going to lie to himself, either: Raines was the right man for the job. If there had been any doubt before, it was gone now.

"Peterson shot Chase, I shot Peterson," Jax said evenly. "And though I didn't witness it personally, Peterson told me he'd also piloted the drones that shot down Air Force One."

The look on the president's face was stony. "You're sure about this, son?"

"Yessir."

"All right, then, I think we're ready to move on. Colonel, could I have a minute with Capt. Booth?"

Archer nodded and made for the door. Raines turned to his Secret Service man and motioned toward the exit. The man raised an eyebrow, but followed suit. Jax was suddenly alone in a room with the President of the United States. Under any other circumstances, it would have been the most memorable moment of his military career.

"Sir," he said.

"What part of the Lone Star State do you hail from, Jax?" Raines asked.

"Northeast, sir. Near Jacksonville. That's where my folks got my name."

Raines grinned. "I thought I caught the east in that drawl. Cattle country. I'm from Houston myself. Most people can't tell because I worked hard to cover it up when I went to Washington, for all the good it did me."

"Yessir."

"Goes without saying your father was a fan of John Wayne."

Now it was Jax's turn to grin. "The Duke was right below Jesus on the totem pole, sir."

"Good, good. I think Texans understand the value of a hero more than most of the country. Like Davy Crockett. Someone larger than life, you know? A fella who can rally folks around a flag."

Jax nodded.

"Take the Alamo," Raines said, turning serious again. "Did you know that there's evidence Crockett didn't die in battle? That he actually was one of the people who surrendered and was executed by Santa Anna's men? They usually leave that part out of the history books, so I wouldn't be surprised if you didn't. There's no way to prove it, one way or the other."

Jax stood in silence. He wasn't sure if the president expected him to speak. After a few moments, Raines continued.

"I guess what I'm saying is it doesn't really matter what happened," he said. "Davy Crockett is still a hero, and 'Remember the

Alamo!' was a rallying cry for a lot of people. To those people, the legend of Davy Crockett was more important than the man."

"Sir?"

"What Col. Archer said is true: Eko was a North Korean weapon against America that took the rest of the world with it. And I can confirm that we've traced whatever the hell that cyber weapon was back to China. Just like Eko, it got out of control and spread. In the past few weeks, Earth has been hit with a perfect storm that's going to wipe out most of the population of the planet and may well set mankind's clock back to the Industrial Age; maybe even further. Our experts estimate it will take at least a century of struggle to recover from this, if we even can."

Jax took a deep, shaky breath. He would have thought it impossible to still feel horror after everything he'd learned in the last half-hour, but he was wrong.

Raines dropped a hand on Jax's shoulder. "Archer is right: America needs an enemy. But I think she also needs a hero. And who better for the job than the brave soldier who killed the enemy saboteur and tried in vain to save one of the greatest Americans who ever lived?"

"Sir."

"One thing is certain, son: whatever happens next, the fate of the republic rests on our shoulders. America has to endure, because if America is over, then the world is over. And the world cannot be over."

8

"Everybody's saluting you," Hayley said as they navigated the corridors of Cheyenne Mountain on their way to Cpl. Brown and the comms room.

Jax had hoped she wouldn't press the issue of finding her grandparents for a while, until he could figure out a way to tell her the truth: that America was halfway down the highway to hell, and it was headed for a steep downward grade any minute now. But here they were, on their way. The best he could hope for was to see her disappointed yet again.

"It's just a way of showing respect," he said. "We don't always do it."

"They didn't do it before. Is it because you shot that bad guy?"

He sighed. Raines had broken the news about Fletcher and Chase via closed circuit broadcast throughout Cheyenne at 0800. The shock soon gave way to almost fawning admiration for Jax. The members of Echo Company had practically mobbed him when he arrived for breakfast after the broadcast; Ruben had managed to restrain himself from busting Jax's balls over the whole thing, and even saluted him.

Maybe Raines was right—maybe people did need a hero in times when everything looked like it was falling apart. That didn't mean Jax was comfortable with it, though.

Thank God he'd told Hayley himself in the women's barracks before the breakfast free-for-all. She took it well, seeming to understand that things weren't the way they had been anymore. He was learning that she was remarkably mature for someone who still had a stuffed panda; he'd noticed with some satisfaction that it was now relegated to a spot under her pillow during the day.

"Yup," he said, returning the salutes of a pair of airmen—male, this time—as he and Hayley turned down the anthill tunnel that led to the comms room. "It'll stop soon."

"How come?"

"Because there are too many other things to think about right now."

"Oh. I guess that makes sense."

They approached the open door to the comms room and saw Cpl. Brown's orange bun behind a bank of screens.

"Corporal," Jax said by way of greeting. "It's us again."

She seemed startled and stood awkwardly, throwing a hand up to her brow in a salute.

"Sir. Sorry, I didn't see you there."

"At ease. How are things going?"

"Uh," she said. "Good. Fine. Everything's fine. Sir."

Her tone told Jax that everything was most definitely *not* fine, which he already knew.

"Did you talk to my grandma and grandpa?" Hayley asked, wide-eyed.

Jax held up a hand. "It's okay if you haven't," he said. "I know how busy you are."

Brown bit her lip. "Actually, I did get a return email from them. Just this morning, in fact."

Hayley's face lit up, but Jax arched an eyebrow. Brown gave him a pleading look, so he decided to let her talk—for now.

"What does it say?" Hayley asked.

"I wish it was better news, honey," the corporal said. "They're stuck where they are. It says: 'Dear Hayley, we're so happy to hear from you. You must be devastated by your mother's death, as we are. We love you so much, and we want to see you. But the roads around our town have been blocked by the police, and no one Is being allowed in or out.'"

The girl's face sagged, but Jax thought she didn't look quite as crushed as she had before.

"It goes on to say: 'We know that Jax is taking good care of you and that you're safe where you are. The world is going a little bit crazy right now, sweetheart, so he's going to need your help to figure things out and make sure that you're okay and happy. And when things go back to normal, we will come and get you as soon as we can. We can't wait to see you and give you lots of hugs and kisses. Stay strong.'"

Brown looked up from the screen. "It signs off: 'Love, Grandma and Grandpa.'"

Hayley's gaze was on the floor. Jax put a hand on her shoulder and knelt beside her.

"I'm sorry," he said. "I guess you're stuck with me for a while longer."

She gave him a half-smile that he was sure she didn't feel. "I'm not 'stuck' with you," she husked. "It's not *that* bad here."

"There are lots of roads that have been closed off," Brown said. "In fact, it sounds like most of the cities have been sealed to make sure that the virus doesn't spread. There are probably tons of kids in the same situation."

The girl nodded. "I guess. Can I send an email back to them?"

Jax and the corporal exchanged a glance.

"Sorry, honey, not right now. We're... having a power brownout right now, so we have to limit messages to just military stuff. I'll send for you as soon as we're able to get through again, okay?"

Hayley nodded, brightening. "Okay." She turned to Jax. "Can I go back to my bunk? Val found some old books for me. Something about travelling pants. I don't know what that's supposed to mean, but she said I'd like them."

He stood and put a hand on her shoulder. "You bet, go on. I need to stay here and talk to Cpl. Brown for a minute."

She nodded, giving Brown a wide smile. "Thank you, Corporal."

The woman returned her smile with a pained one of her own. "Anytime, sweetie."

They watched the girl disappear down the corridor. When she was out of sight, Jax turned to Brown.

"That didn't come from the Townshends, did it?"

Her pale cheeks filled with color and she looked down at the desk. "I'm sorry, sir, I just couldn't..."

"It's all right," he said, holding up a hand to quiet her. "More than all right, it was incredibly kind. Thank you."

She nodded silently.

"How bad is it?" he asked.

"We're getting nothing back from anywhere," she said. "The Internet is completely out. Analog military channels are nothing but static. If we're this quiet *here*, at Cheyenne? The rest of the country doesn't have a hope of communicating with each other."

Jax nodded, frowning. "It's going to get worse. And soon."

"I know. I saw the vice—I mean the president's message. About what happened with you and Secretary Chase. It's crazy."

More crazy than you know, he thought.

"Do you think there are more of them?" she asked. "Enemy agents, I mean? Here in Cheyenne?"

"No." That much was true. "There was only one. He was enough."

"Yessir."

"Keep your chin up, Corporal," he said as he headed to the door. "We'll get through this. And thank you again. I owe you one."

"We all owe *you* one, sir," she said, sitting back down in front of her screens.

He nodded and headed into the corridor. The lie was already getting easier.

9

The drive from the mountain base to Cheyenne Mountain Resort told Jax even more than his conversation with Cpl. Brown had the day before: shit was most definitely full-on sideways. So sideways, in fact, that he wondered if Raines's words about things taking a century of struggle to get right again might have been overly optimistic.

Outside the windows of the Yukon, he saw hundreds of vehicles lining virtually every square foot of the shoulder on both sides of Highway 115 and the median in between. The road bisected the east side of Colorado Springs and was a major artery through the city. Crews had obviously been working around the clock to clear the road, but their driver still had to creep along in certain spots to avoid the vehicles that hadn't made it all the way off the asphalt.

"Takes your breath away, doesn't it?" Archer said from his seat beside Jax.

Jax shook his head. "Why would they bother trying to leave?"

"Instinct. We're wired for fight or flight, and you can't fight a disease. Ergo, you try to run away from it."

"And end up making everything that much worse."

Archer sighed. "I don't think it makes much of a difference. If people die in their beds or in a car in a traffic jam on the freeway, the result is still the same."

"Except for the survivors," said Jax. "They're the ones who have to deal with it all."

The colonel looked him in the eye, and Jax couldn't miss the rebuke in that gaze.

"I think you missed the keyword in what you just said, Captain. *Survivors.*"

Jax looked away, suddenly ashamed. Archer was right: who was he, or any of them, to complain about the cards they'd been dealt? They were *alive*. Thousands around them weren't. And if what Raines had said was accurate, the number of dead beyond the relative safety of this little piece of the Rockies would be in the hundreds of millions. Billions, when you counted outside of the United States.

Suburban neighborhoods gleamed in the late summer sunshine outside the van's windows. Hundreds of miniature castles protected by vinyl siding and separated by tall cedar fences, the kind that made good neighbors. If not for the vehicles on the side of the road, Jax could have almost believed that nothing had changed in the world.

Now he wondered how many victims of Eko were slowly rotting behind the walls of those affordable tract homes. How many parents held the lifeless bodies of their children in their laps as they themselves succumbed to their symptoms: fever, hallucinations, a crushing headache. How many of them were already lying in a pool of their own shit as the last of their life drained out of them?

The thought dragged memories to the surface of Rachel in her sickbed at the hospice in Boblingen. Her gray skin, her gray eyes. Had it really been only a week ago?

Back then, he thought she had won some sort of reverse lottery by being one of the first exposed to Eko. Her death was a horrible, infuriating injustice against him and Hayley, something they alone would have to endure, and that no one else would be able to understand.

Now he realized the whole world was joining in their pain, only instead of just watching their loved ones die, they were dying right alongside them.

He and Archer rode in silence the rest of the way to the resort. Jax took note of the upscale neighborhood that surrounded it, deserted now, and the guards at the gate. What had no doubt been a bustling parking lot less than two weeks ago was now empty except for a dozen or so dun-colored Humvees and black SUVs.

Behind the resort, Cheyenne Mountain rose like a protective mother. Jax was already starting to think of the base underneath it as home, which would have been depressing if he'd allowed himself time to dwell on it.

Archer led him through the entrance and past a number of conference rooms. The place was buzzing with people in fatigues, carrying papers and talking into radios. Finally the colonel led him through a door and into a well-appointed room that looked like a rich outdoorsman's man cave. The walls were lined in burnished pine, the floor covered in an ornate hunter-green carpet. A stone fireplace dominated the space between the windows on the wall, and a pair of overstuffed armchairs faced a matching sofa across a solid ebony coffee table.

To the right was a conference table with chairs and a coffee service. Three people were already seated: a swarthy man in his forties with a shaved head, a nervous-looking middle-aged man and a young woman with strawberry blond hair and a barely suppressed scowl, all wearing different styles of fatigues.

Archer motioned Jax to a chair at the table. "Major Brian Price from the marines and Major Alfred Skolnik, ranking member of the Colorado National Guard, I'd like you to meet Capt. Jackson Booth, 10th Special Forces Group."

The men looked mildly surprised as they shook Jax's hand. *Word travels fast*, he thought.

Archer turned to the woman. "And this is definitely *not* Col. Nicholas Roth, ranking member of the air force in El Paso County."

She rose and saluted. "Lt. Carly Grant, sir. Col. Roth sends his apologies."

"And a surrogate."

"He's tied up with aircraft maintenance issues, and he thought my experience in health care would allow me to be of service, sir. I was a civilian nurse before I signed up."

"Then Col. Roth obviously hasn't been paying attention to what's been going on," Archer said as he motioned for them all to take a seat. "Pardon me for saying, Lieutenant, but I don't see us doing much flying when every computer in the fucking country is essentially a paperweight. And I would have thought that anyone with medical training would be of more use tending to the thousands of airmen at your bases currently in the throes of the Eko virus. I know Fort Carson could use every hand they can get right now."

Blood rushed into the lieutenant's pale cheeks, but she said nothing.

"Let me bring you up to speed," said Archer. "I'm sure word has reached your various camps that Colton Raines is now the president, and that Marcus Chase is dead."

They nodded as all eyes landed on Jax, prompting an uncomfortable twinge in his belly.

"Cheyenne Mountain will be the seat of government and the HQ of all military operations for the foreseeable future," Archer continued. "President Raines has tasked me with coordinating the remaining military here in Colorado Springs. The army is running the show at the mountain. There'll be more details about the command structure soon."

The others eyed each other nervously. Jax couldn't blame them—the different branches weren't known for playing nice with each other. But they had no choice in this situation. The marines and navy were far from here, and the national guard was barely a thing in Colorado, thanks to the huge number of active military members. The air force had a strong presence in the Springs, but, as Archer pointed out, what were they going to fly?

And the burning question now was: how many military personnel were left?

"I'll be blunt," said Archer. "For all intents and purposes, you're all in the army now. Official orders are being drafted as we speak."

The others at the table looked at each other, then at Jax, and finally back to Archer.

"Sir, if I may?" said Grant. "Is that why you brought us to the resort? Word is that it's going to be used by the top brass."

He nodded. "Exactly. You'll also be given quarters here immediately."

"Nice work if you can get it," said Skolnik, the national guard man. "The place is pretty swanky. I guess rank has its privileges, hey?"

Archer leveled a gaze at the man. "Actually, we're using it because you have to travel through the heart of Colorado Springs to get here, Major. Cheyenne Mountain Complex is isolated and protected. This resort isn't—it's right in the middle of the death and destruction. The president thought it was important for his commanders to see it close up, all the time. That's why he's staying here, too."

Skolnik's thinning hair dropped into his line of sight as his eyes widened.

"Hey, I didn't mean—"

"You were a reservist, correct, Major?" Archer asked.

The man nodded.

"Then let me do you a favor and loop you in on what's happening here. The big dogs are running shit, and the national guard, or whatever is left of it here, will be answering to them."

"But President Fletcher said—"

"I reiterate, Major, that Colton Raines is now the commander-in-chief. And he says you all work for us. As for the rest of America outside the walls of this valley, I regret to say that they are on their own as of now. Colorado Springs *is* the new republic."

He gave that a moment to sink in. Price was nodding, Grant looked shocked. Jax thought Skolnik looked ready to vomit.

"I didn't sign up for this kind of shit," Skolnik said. "I'm an accountant, for Christ's sake. It was only supposed to be weekends! Then a few days ago they gave me a needle and told me I was a major. Ever since then, I've been shuttled from one place to another, but no one ever gave me any orders!"

Archer nodded. "I'm about to get to that. The guard doesn't have much of a presence in Colorado Springs because the army and air force are so prevalent here. Not to put too fine a point on it, Major, but you're a figurehead."

He turned to Jax. "Capt. Booth here has been assigned a unique duty. He'll be the liaison between Cheyenne Mountain and the public of Colorado Springs. We need to start building a bridge between the military and the civilian population if we're going to have a hope of surviving this with a minimum amount of chaos.

"That's where you three will come in—I need you to be representatives of your branches, and to be seen with Capt. Booth here. One big, happy military family that's here to help."

Jax had been briefed on what this meeting would be about, but hearing his new role described in such a way suddenly made him feel like a fraud. He was a fighter, not a bridge-builder. Point him at the bad guys and order him to kill, fine. Point him at the public and tell him to *liaise* and *build consensus*? He didn't know if he was up to it.

Then again, if not him, then who?

"Excuse me, sir," said Grant. "Can I assume you meant this role is for Col. Roth?"

"Not anymore," said Archer. "At first, yes. Now I can see the value of having a female on the team. And one with medical training will be that much better."

Her eyebrows went up. "You're saying...?"

"You represent the air force, and you answer to Capt. Booth. As of right now."

She blinked at him for a moment. "And what should I tell Col. Roth, sir?"

"Tell him if he has a problem with me, he can fucking well meet me in person instead of being a passive-aggressive pussy and sending subordinates to his meetings. Now, if we're all on the same page, I'm going to turn you over to Capt. Booth. I've got other meetings to get to."

The colonel gathered up his papers. As he passed Jax on the way to the door, he nodded.

"They're all yours, Captain."

"Sir." The word felt like sand against his suddenly dry vocal cords.

The door opened and closed, leaving Jax in the room with his three new colleagues. They were all looking at him with a mix of suspicion and confusion. There was also more than a little anger in Lt. Grant's blue eyes.

He looked at them all with what he hoped was an air of confidence that he didn't feel.

"All right, then," he said in his most authoritative voice. "Let's get down to business."

10

It felt good to have Ruben and Cruz with him again, even if their duty today was something none of them were prepared for. But then, how could anyone be prepared for it? They didn't teach post-apocalyptic urban management in any army training course Jax had ever heard of.

The Hummer cruised slowly down East Boulder Street through the heart of Colorado Springs. Stately old homes, some of which had been subdivided into jaunty apartments, shared space with strip malls housing everything from restaurants to architects to used book stores. It was the kind of place Jax could have seen himself settling down in with Rachel and Hayley if the world hadn't decided to end.

"This is creepy," Ruben said from the backseat. "I mean, it's a beautiful day, the sun is shining, and yet there's no one on the street anywhere. Just empty cars."

"It's like a movie set that's been abandoned," Val said.

"A lot of the people are in the makeshift hospices that have been set up at the schools and at Fort Carson," said Jax. "Archer says the number of people entering the final stages of Eko has increased a hundredfold in the last few days. That includes a lot of the people who've been acting as caregivers."

Ruben let out a low whistle. "Jesus. All while we've been sitting under a mountain."

Jax made the mistake of glancing into the front seat of a parked Jeep as he drove past. A gray figure—he couldn't tell if it was a man or a woman—was slumped over the steering wheel, a cloud of flies crawling in the pool of blood left on the dashboard. Whatever that person had been in life, he or she had died alone in their car, probably reeking of their own shit. His stomach threatened to rebel, but he clamped down against it.

They drove on, followed closely by a second Hummer with Grant, Price and Skolnik in it. Jax wondered if Skolnik would make it through the day without suffering a nervous breakdown. He wasn't made for the kind of work they were about to begin.

Still, the four had managed to come up with a skeleton of a plan over the past twenty-four hours. Jax had chosen William J. Palmer High School, a few blocks ahead of them, because it was close to the center of town. He didn't want to be seen as favoring any particular area of the city, and he wanted to draw as many people to this thing as he could, so the central location was best.

I'm already thinking like a politician, he thought as he turned onto North Weber and pulled up in front of the entrance to the school. The other Hummer parked behind them on the street.

"Nice school," Ruben said as they got out and stood on the sidewalk. The entrance was a grid of glass protected from the sun by a ramada held up by four brick pillars. "Far cry from the ones I went to in South Central."

"You mean the ones you *skipped out* from in South Central," Jax said.

Ruben flipped him the bird as they approached the door. "Doesn't look like there's anyone here, students or teachers."

Cruz reported in to Cheyenne on her walkie. As she did, Price, Skolnik and Grant joined them in the foyer.

"Home of the Terrors," said Grant, pointing to a banner of an eagle talon hanging on a wall. "Anybody else see that as oddly prophetic?"

"This was my school," Skolnik said absently. "Good old brown and white. Lance Armstrong went here when I was here. I didn't know him personally, though." He paused. "I wonder if he's dead now."

"Let's focus on the task at hand," said Jax.

Price nodded. "He's telling you to shut up, Skolnik. You're not bringing anything to this party; just stay out of the way."

"I don't recall asking for an interpreter, Major," Jax said evenly. It was a calculated shot: the Marine outranked him, but Archer had put Jax in charge of this team, and he knew if he gave Price free rein, he would try to take over. The man was a jarhead right down to his DNA.

Price's eyes flashed for a moment and Jax prepared for a confrontation. He knew he'd win a physical fight, especially with Ruben and Val to back him up, but he hoped it wouldn't come to that.

After a few tense beats, Price gave a curt nod. The rest of the crew relaxed noticeably.

Crisis One averted, Jax thought. *Only a few million more to go.*

They followed the halls to the main gymnasium. As they entered, they could see the bleachers had been pulled out and a pair of tables set side-by-side on a dais. In front of the tables was a lectern with a microphone.

"Hello!" a female voice called. Jax saw a compact, middle-aged woman in a pink sweatsuit emerge from the doorway to the hall on the other side of the room.

"Ma'am," he said. "I'm Capt. Jackson Booth. We're here from Cheyenne Mountain."

The woman hurried across the gym floor with her arm outstretched.

"Yes, yes, yes," she burbled, pumping his hand. "Carol Firth. I'm with the PTA. The treasurer. Maggie said you were coming. Thank God you're here. Thank God, thank God, thank God." She finished up with a wild-eyed giggle.

Jax nodded. "I'm sorry, Maggie is...?"

"Maggie Stubbs." She blinked. "The new sheriff."

"I'm sorry, I was told we were to meet Police Chief Monroe."

The woman's face tightened into a manic mask. "Yeah, about that," she said, shaking her head. "He's sick. Yup, under the weather. Lot of people getting sick these days! Not good. Not good, not good, not good." A comical sigh.

The team exchanged glances with Jax.

"It's all right, Carol," said a voice from behind them.

Jax turned to see a woman about his age, tall, with chestnut hair pulled back in a serious bun. Her uniform was made up of a light gray shirt and dark gray pants, with black flaps on the shirt pockets. Even without the pistol on her hip, Jax could tell who she was.

"Sheriff Stubbs," he said. "Capt. Jackson Booth."

"I assumed as much." The clicking of her boot heels echoed through the gym as she walked toward them.

"Thank you for getting the word out about this meeting. These are my colleagues—"

"Pardon my French, Captain, but I don't give a shit about your colleagues." She turned to them. "No offense, but If you're not here to work for me, I don't need to know who you are."

Carol Firth cleared her throat loudly. "I'm just going to go make coffee," she declared, scurrying out the way she'd come in.

Great, Jax thought. *Amateur hour.*

"Look, Sheriff, I understand you've been under stress—"

"Stress?" she barked. "Captain, while you've been sitting under that fucking mountain, this city has been going to hell. Despite what Carol seems to have told herself, as of last night, Ted Monroe is *dead.* So is the mayor. And Kenny Clayton, the man who was my sheriff up until a couple of days ago. I was appointed by the last El Paso County Commissioner who wasn't confined to a bed at Fort Carson. She was sick then; I don't know what her condition is now. I would've thought you'd know all of this."

"Unfortunately, we're not getting regular updates from the city—"

"Is that right? Well, pardon all of us for not taking time out of our day to send you our itineraries. Oh wait, we have no means of doing that. Silly me."

"Sheriff," Jax said firmly. "We're here to help."

Her icy glare told him those weren't the words Maggie Stubbs wanted to hear.

"How do you plan to do that, exactly?" she asked. "The last thing the president said on the TV was that the national guard was in charge, which around here means the army and air force. They did help, for a few days. They were getting people out to the makeshift hospitals, clearing the roads, but no one seemed to know who was in charge. And every day, there've been fewer and fewer of them showing up."

Jax nodded. Archer had managed to get a more comprehensive report on the state of the Springs and the surrounding bases earlier that morning. The area was home to one of the largest military populations in the country, but fewer than eight percent of them had been vaccinated against Eko, and that had been with an experimental earlier version, X-54, which had proved less than 50 percent effective. Those numbers boiled down to an ugly picture: by the time the pandemic was over (assuming it *would* end; there was no guarantee of that), there would be approximately twelve hundred healthy soldiers and airmen left out of more than forty-five thousand a month earlier.

Fort Carson was essentially a hospice for the dying: every bed full, every floor surface covered with whatever soft material could be found, trying to make them comfortable. One of the biggest drains on the remaining manpower would soon be digging mass graves.

Jax now had the task of figuring out how much of that he should tell the civilian public. He and his own soldiers had a hard enough time processing the information themselves.

"You're right, it's a shit show," he admitted. "I'm not going to stand here and pretend that everything's okay, Sheriff. We're in the mother of all emergency situations, and that's not going to change anytime soon. I understand how hard it's been on you first responders."

"Do you?" she asked. "Paramedics and nurses are working round the clock. I have two deputies left on active duty; I think there are a dozen city cops who aren't too sick to work yet. Banks have been closed for days now, people are abandoning their businesses, the government has shut down, all the public buildings are empty. I'm amazed we haven't seen wide-scale looting yet."

"It's coming," said Jax. "That's why we're having this meeting. To let people know how things are going to proceed from this point."

She crossed her arms over her chest. "So how *are* they going to proceed, Capt. Booth? I'm dying to know."

Jax glanced around at his team. Price met his gaze with raised eyebrows: *this is your show, buddy.*

"Maybe you should sit down," Jax said.

"I haven't sat down in a week," she said. "Just talk."

He took a deep breath, let it out. "All right, then, here's the Cliff Notes version: President Fletcher is dead. Air Force One was shot down en route to Cheyenne by a drone piloted by someone working for the Chinese government, who then went on to murder Defense Secretary Chase before I took him out."

He still winced inwardly at the lie as the sheriff's eyes widened.

"Colton Raines is now president, and he's here in Colorado Springs, along with as many surviving military leaders as could be rounded up, outside of the navy. We can't get them here, for obvious reasons, so they've been left out of the equation."

Stubbs's eyes widened. "So it's true? There's no air travel? Not even military?"

"If I may, sir?" Lt. Grant said, raising a hand. Jax nodded. "Sheriff, I'm with the air force. The cyber attack that shut down most computers in the country has had an effect on almost all electronics. We might be able to get planes in the air, but there's no way to pilot them properly without a cohesive support system on the ground. There's a possibility we might be able to mobilize some decommissioned aircraft in the future, but that's a long way off."

"Jesus," Stubbs breathed. "We thought—hoped, I guess—that the electronics problem was localized somehow. You're saying it's nationwide?"

"Our best intel suggests it's worldwide," said Jax. "A targeted cyber weapon from China that went rogue and infected everything it came in contact with. Just like Eko, courtesy of North Korea."

She ran a hand down her face. "It's a perfect storm."

He nodded. "A storm we have to weather, and soon we'll have to clean up the aftermath. Now, I hope it's something we can all do together. But part of the reason I'm here is to make it clear to the civilian public that the army is in charge from this point on, and that we'll need their help."

At that moment, Jax registered movement from the main entrance as a dozen or more men marched into the gymnasium, ranging in age from early twenties to late middle age. Each was carrying at least one rifle; several had bandoliers strapped across their chests and holstered pistols on each hip.

"That's good to hear," said one of them, a white-haired man in camouflage hunting gear. "'Cause we were looking to talk about that particular subject ourselves."

11

"Gentlemen," Jax said. "Welcome. It's good to see you."

He could feel Ruben tensing beside him, and assumed the same from Cruz and Price. They were fighters, and they'd just registered a threat. Jax casually flexed a hand behind his back, hoping the three would take it as a signal to stand down.

"You got a permit for those?" the sheriff asked.

Jax forced himself to chuckle, despite the screw that was twisting in his guts. "That's a good one, Maggie. Come on in, fellas, have a seat. Coffee should be ready in a minute."

The men looked at each other before following the suggestion and sitting down on the first row of the bleachers. As they talked in hushed tones, Jax gathered his people around him.

"I don't like—" Maggie began before Jax cut her off.

"Stow it," he said with quiet force. "I'm in charge here. Lambert, Cruz, take the three and nine position. Be ready to draw on my signal. Major Price, stick by the door. Same orders."

He turned to Skolnik and Grant. "Get back to the Hummer. You know what to do. Three hits on the radio. If you don't hear that, you don't do a thing."

Grant nodded while Skolnik turned green. They walked toward the exit, making an effort to look casual.

"Laugh," Jax said to Maggie.

"What?"

"I said laugh, like I just made a joke. We're all friends here. And if they want to carry their guns, that's what we're going to let them do. We're not going to make an issue of it—yet."

She blinked at him several times before letting out a strained chuckle. Val and Ruben ambled toward opposite sides of the bleachers as Jax placed a hand on Maggie's back and led her along with him to the dais.

A larger crowd started streaming into the gym as Price headed to take his position at the door. Many of them had hunting rifles slung over their shoulders, including some of the women. A couple of older gentlemen were drinking beer from cans they'd pulled from the six-packs dangling from their other hands.

"I should have realized they'd come armed," Maggie said as they stood next to the lectern. "We haven't seen much resistance to authority up till now; I should have known it wouldn't be long."

"That's what we're here to try and prevent," said Jax.

"Good luck with that."

He gave her a half smile. "Keep hope alive, Sheriff."

They waited for the new arrivals to settle in. Carol Firth had reappeared and was scurrying around setting up a folding table under the basketball net with two large metal coffee urns. She placed boxes of sugar cubes next to large shakers of off-white powder, the kind that left a skein of ivory scum on the surface. People lined up on both ends to get their Styrofoam cups of sludge. Jax wondered absently how long they could expect the power to stay on—hot coffee might be a luxury sooner than any of them realized.

He nodded to Ruben and Val in their positions, then to Price at the door. Time to get this show on the road.

"Good afternoon, ladies and gentlemen," he said into the microphone. It let out a whine of feedback, prompting a manic giggle from Carol Firth.

"Who the hell are you?" a man yelled from one of the middle rows. A susurrus of agreement ran through the crowd; apparently, they all wanted to know who the hell he was.

"My name is Jackson Booth, Captain, United States Army Special Forces. With me here is Maggie Stubbs, the newly appointed sheriff of El Paso County."

"Good for you," said another voice, female this time. "What the fuck is going on?"

More agreement, louder this time. Jax couldn't blame them—what else would you expect from people who had been through what they had?

"I'm going to do my best to answer your questions," he said. "And I have a few for you, as well. I think we can all agree that we're going to have to work together to get through the days ahead."

"My wife is dying in a cot up at Fort Carson!" the first man said. The angry red circles around his eyes hinted that he hadn't slept in days. "How's she gonna get through?"

"I'm very sorry, sir. The government is doing all it can to deal with the situation, but it's been far worse than we first realized. As much as I'd like to not be the one to bring you this news, I'm afraid we no longer have the luxury to be anything other than brutally frank. It pains me to say this, sir, but the vast majority of people now sick with the virus will not recover."

Another susurrus, louder this time. Jax doubted he was telling anyone in the room anything they hadn't already suspected deep down, but it would still be jarring. He'd felt the same way when Archer had first brought him up to speed.

"Our first responders have been doing an admirable job helping the public and maintaining order," he said, motioning to Maggie. "They've been working night and day alongside our military personnel. No doubt you've seen them throughout the city."

"I seen 'em drive by people who needed help!" an older man shouted. "Like they wasn't even there!"

Jax nodded. "We've had to prioritize due to dwindling numbers.

Only a fraction of first responders and soldiers are available for duty; we're losing our people to the virus, too."

"When is the vaccine coming?" This was followed by a number of people crossing their arms over their chests. A few clutched their hands in front of them, as if in prayer.

"As I said, this is a time to be brutally frank," Jax said somberly. "The truth is that the virus—it was named Eko by the Center for Disease Control—struck too quickly for the CDC to catch it. By the time they had developed the X-57 vaccine, the virus had already spread globally. It was already impossible to get ahead of it."

A number of people asked a version of the same question at the same time: "Where did it come from?"

"Fucking Africa!" one long-haired man hollered. "I seen it online before the Internet crapped out!"

"Shut up!" a woman yelled back. "Let the man talk!"

Jax gripped the sides of the lectern. "You have a right to know everything," he said.

He spent the next few minutes bringing the crowd up to speed with the events of the past several days, including the legend of Jax Booth, saboteur killer, and the evil Chinese empire. And the fact that supplies of X-57 had run out.

"President Raines was adamant that we keep the public informed of the threat that our nation faces," he said. "It's imperative that America make it through this situation, and to do that, we must band together."

Jax noticed a number of people turning to glare at a young Asian man in the audience. He returned their looks, wide-eyed.

"Are you fucking kidding me?" the man cried. "I grew up here! I went to *this school* with some of you!"

"The enemy isn't here," Jax said sternly. "They struck from a distance, and they themselves are now dealing with the effects of their own attacks. All of our intelligence says that there's no place in the developed world that hasn't been equally affected. This... *collapse* is worldwide."

"Is that supposed to make us feel better?" a man asked bleakly.

"No. Nothing will do that at this stage, and things are only going to get worse."

"Then what *are* you here to say?" Maggie asked from beside him. It was genuine curiosity he heard in her voice now, not sarcasm.

Nods and agreement from the crowd. Jax checked his three guards again before reaching a hand casually down to his belt to turn on his walkie.

"Some sixty-five years ago," he said, "John F. Kennedy told the American people to ask not what their country could do for them, but what they could do for their country. At the time, it was meant to encourage citizens to get involved in their community."

He plucked the microphone from the stand and stepped down from the dais. He saw Ruben and Val tense as he did, but he doubted anyone else would notice. In a few steps, he was standing only a few yards from the bleachers.

"Today, President Raines is challenging you to make that same commitment: to do whatever you can to help America survive this horrible attack. These darkest, most challenging of days. It's more than just rhetoric now—it's absolutely imperative to the survival of our republic."

Christ, I sound like fucking Nixon, he thought, his stomach clenching.

But it seemed to work. No one said a word, just looked at each other, then back to Jax. A few clasped their hands under their chins or ran their hands through their hair. All of them appeared deep in thought.

He'd struck a chord with that line. Hit the people where they lived. For one brief, shining moment, the future looked clear.

Then it all blew up in his face.

12

"I think you're full of shit," said the white-haired man who had been the first to speak from the original armed contingent that had shown up early. "You're just looking for us to kowtow to you army fuckers!"

"Shut up, moron!" another man yelled. "You're the one who's full of shit!"

"You want to watch your mouth," the white-haired man said, dropping his hand to the pistol on his belt.

"Okay, let's dial it back," said Jax, raising his hands. "This is supposed to be—"

White Hair cut him off. "I *know* what it's supposed to be; it's *these* idiots who don't know. Be honest, *Captain*." He said it with a sneer in his voice. "You're here to tell us the army is in charge of everything. Go ahead and tell me that's not true."

Alarm was starting to creep across Maggie's face. At three and nine, Ruben and Val were squaring their stance and moving their right hands to their weapons. By the door, Jax could see the cords on Price's neck standing out.

"A central authority is crucial—" he began.

"Central authority!" White Hair hooted. "Yeah, I heard that

before. That's what the socialist regimes used to tell people in banana republics before they started grinding them under their boot heels!"

"Sir, you need to calm down," Maggie said from behind Jax. He could hear the natural air of authority in her voice. "This is supposed to be a civil meeting. If you don't sit down, I'll be forced to charge you with disturbing the peace."

The men around White Hair began to snicker. He himself held up his hands as if to surrender.

"You gonna lock me up, Sheriff?" he asked in a mocking tone. "'Cause I only see one of you."

Before anyone could speak, Jax covered the ten feet between him and the white-haired man in three strides, until their faces were only inches apart. The man's shocked expression would have been comical under other circumstances.

"STAND DOWN!" Jax bellowed straight from his diaphragm, startling the man backwards until he tripped over the bleachers and went sprawling on his ass.

Some of the crowd erupted in laughter. Unfortunately, Jax saw, the original armed contingent weren't among them. He felt a blade of adrenaline slice through his belly as they started to unshoulder their weapons. A few had shotguns, but what concerned him were the handful of AR-15s. The rifles were semi-auto, but could have easily—if illegally—been modified to full auto. He doubted that was the case, but he couldn't be sure about anything these days.

White Hair scrambled to his feet and pulled a nine-millimeter from the holster on his waist.

"You're gonna take this from my cold dead hand," he spat. "The Constitution warned us about letting ourselves be taken over by armies."

"You're insane!" a woman cried out. "They're here to help!"

"Oh, they're *always* here to help," said White Hair. "Next thing you know their boots are on your throat. Not me, sister."

Several of the rest of the crowd started to make their way to the door. Out of the corner of his eye, Jax saw Price advancing into the room from the doorway, hand on his holster. At three and nine, Ruben and Val were doing the same.

The eerie calm that Jax always felt in combat swept over him like a cool wave. This he was familiar with.

"Drop your weapons," he commanded. "Now."

"Or what?" asked one of the others, a muscular man in his early twenties who was now pointing his Remington over-under at Jax's chest.

"Or you won't have to worry about Eko," said a female voice.

Jax glanced over to see that Maggie had somehow managed to approach the kid from his flank without being seen, and was now pointing the barrel of her service revolver at his head. *Shit.*

Jax reached down to the radio on his belt and hit the squelch button three times.

"We can end this right now," he said evenly. "Everyone lowers their weapon. No one needs to get hurt here."

"Answer the question!" a man shouted from the crowd. He wasn't part of the armed contingent, but the anger of his face was obvious. "Or *what*? What if we don't go along with you? We got our rights! Like he said, it's in the Constitution!"

More murmurs of agreement in the group. Jax squeezed his eyes shut and hissed out a breath. He wished it hadn't come to this. But deep inside, hadn't he always known it would?

"President Fletcher's last act as commander-in-chief was to declare a state of martial law across the United States," he said evenly. "The military is the final authority in the country until further notice."

On cue, he saw Ruben, Val and Price draw their weapons. He stepped forward, ignoring the shotgun pointed at him.

"Jesus Christ!" someone yelled. The crowd was agitated now.

Jax raised his voice but kept it under control. *"This is the new reality,"* he called. "And at the risk of putting too fine a point on things, if you're a civilian, you are either *on* the bus or you are *under* the bus. Is that clear?"

Things went to hell quickly after that: one of the armed contingent leapt from the third riser of the bleacher and tackled Maggie to the gym floor, which allowed the man she'd been holding her weapon on to raise his shotgun to a spot between Jax's eyes.

Two things happened immediately after that. First, Ruben put a bullet between the shoulders of the white-haired man, who had crawled his way back to the front of the bleachers and thumbed back the hammer of his old nine-millimeter, preparing to fire at Jax.

An instant later, Jax pivoted to his right and brought his right arm up and around in an arc that knocked the barrel of the younger man's Remington away from him. He followed through on the movement, trapping the barrel under his right arm and driving his left elbow into the kid's nose.

Jax was dimly aware of shouts around him as some of the crowd stumbled over each other trying to get out of the way. He was focused on the ten or so men who had showed up armed. They were all in various stages of drawing their weapons; it was obvious none had been properly trained, but there was no doubt what was going to happen next.

He had only a fraction of a second to decide as Archer's words came back to him: *Are you ready to point your weapons at your fellow citizens on American soil, Jax?*

God help him, he was. He was a soldier, and a soldier did his duty, come hell or high water.

Maggie moved to get to her knees, but Jax kicked her back down to the floor with the sole of his boot, drawing his own sidearm at the same time. Two taps later and the kid with the shotgun was jigging backwards into the third riser. Meanwhile, one of the men in camouflage had turned to face Cruz and was squeezing off rounds from his AR-15. The sound of the shots echoed off the high walls as the sergeant returned fire and dropped him with three rounds to the head and throat.

"Motherfucker!" another of the dozen hollered, raising his rifle in Ruben's direction, but it was too late. He was down before he even got the stock into the crook of his shoulder.

Jax dropped to the floor, covering Maggie's body with his own as the rest of White Hair's allies started firing in earnest. From his position, he could see Ruben and Val diving for cover behind the risers as Price walked calmly toward the shooters, firing steadily. Jax thought the major was either the stupidest military man he'd ever seen or the craziest.

"We have to get out of here!" Maggie yelled from under him.

"Stay put!" he ordered.

Two seconds later, he saw what he had been waiting for: Grant had sent in the half-dozen members of Echo Company who had been positioned outside the school. They converged on the gymnasium, firing high-caliber weapons at every armed civilian in the bleachers. They were the best shots in Echo, and Jax knew they would do everything in their power to keep anyone without a weapon from being hurt.

The ad hoc militia lasted about eight seconds against Echo. Jax watched as a stray round shattered the backboard of the basketball net, raining tempered glass down on Carol Firth's coffee urns. A few rounds chewed chunks out of the plaster in the gym walls. When the shooting was over, there were a dozen bodies draped over the risers. Two dozen more people huddled, unharmed but screaming, in various spots between the bleachers and the entrance. Another forty or so had fled the building during the melee.

Jax made a quick scan of the battlefield: Ruben and Val were unhurt. Price was nursing a bleeding bicep, but he was standing.

An Echo corporal named Farries advanced on him. "Sir!" he called. "All clear?"

"All clear," he said, pushing himself off the floor. He reached down and offered a hand to Maggie Stubbs, who took it shakily.

"Jesus Christ," she breathed. "That was... that was..."

"That was regrettable," Jax said with a frown.

With the shooting over, the rest of the crowd bolted frantically for the doorway. A part of Jax wished he could do the same—as much as he knew he'd had no choice but to do what they did, he also knew he'd essentially just wiped his ass with the Constitution. Martial law or not, those men had every right to show up armed and ask hard questions.

Deep down, he knew he'd made the right call. That didn't make what they'd done right—not by a long stretch—but what choice did they have? Order had to be maintained at any cost or Colorado Springs would descend into chaos, and once they started down that road, there was no hope for America.

"Regrettable?" Maggie's eyes widened. "You just killed a dozen civilians!"

He rounded on her. "That's one way to look at it," he said coldly. "Another is that we just stopped a dozen armed civilians from making a mistake that could have cost the lives of every last person in the room."

Maggie shook her head. "You know that's crazy, right?"

"It sure is," he said. "Welcome to the new republic."

Then he pulled out his radio and sent a message to the resort to get Archer on the line ASAP.

13

The green carpet of the resort meeting room was particularly ugly in the fading light of the afternoon as Jax went over his story in his head. Every angle, every possible outcome, every what-if. Whoever was coming to debrief him on the high school incident—he assumed it would be Archer—wouldn't see any remorse in his eyes. He'd dealt with the situation in the only way he could have.

When he finally heard the sound of the door handle turning, he stood and prepared to salute his colonel. But the man entering the room wasn't Archer.

It was the major from Atlanta.

"Captain," he said, dropping a stack of papers on the conference table. "Sorry I kept you waiting."

Jax noticed the man's hair had been trimmed since he last saw him. "Sir," he said with a salute. "I was expecting Col. Archer."

"I know you were." He motioned for Jax to sit. "Plans have changed. I'm Major Smith. Pleased to meet you."

The man's tone suggested he couldn't care less about meeting Jax. What was this about? He was supposed to be debriefed, and Jax had some pointed questions about the direction he was expected to take going forward. He'd worked out a long, detailed explanation of his actions at the school, and was prepared to argue in his defense.

Now he was in the room with a man he didn't trust as far as he could throw, and he had no idea how much Smith knew about what he'd been discussing with Archer and the president up till now. He wanted to speak, but he wasn't about to offer information to this guy. Not a hope in hell.

The major scanned a piece of paper—Jax saw it was the handwritten report he'd submitted—for several long moments before finally looking him in the eye.

"Anything unusual to report?" the major asked.

The line reminded Jax of the bland way Smith had reacted to learning Hayley would be joining the transport from Stuttgart. That wasn't what he'd expected to hear at all.

"Sir?"

"This summary is pretty straightforward to me," Smith said. "Civilians brought weapons to a public meeting and threatened army personnel. You utilized appropriate specialists to eliminate the threat with minimal consequences. Anything else to add?"

He had plenty to add, but didn't know how far he could go with Smith.

"We were assisted by the El Paso County sheriff," he said. "I think she could be an asset going forward. She's smart and capable."

"Has she been vaccinated?" Smith might as well have been asking about the soup of the day.

"Not that I know of, but she appears to be healthy."

He nodded. "If she hasn't started to show symptoms by now, chances are she's one of the lucky few who are naturally immune. In any case, go ahead and draft her if you think she'll be of use."

Jax cocked an eyebrow. "What if she doesn't *want* to be drafted?"

"No one *wants* to be drafted, Captain. That's why they came up with a different word from 'enlisted'."

Jax couldn't argue with that. His gut cramped at the thought of passing along the news to her. He'd make a point of shielding his groin when he did.

Smith shrugged. "Anything else to add?"

Jax took a deep breath. He needed to take a step further here, consequences be damned.

"To be honest, sir, I expected a little more pushback about my decisions this afternoon."

For the first and only time since Jax had met the man, Smith smiled. Even more surprising, he leaned back in his chair and clasped his hands behind his head.

"President Raines and Col. Archer both sing your praises, Captain," he said. "I can see why. You don't have any illusions about the situation the republic is in, and you apparently understand the old proverb that he who hesitates is lost."

Jax felt a brief surge of pride in spite of himself. He wondered if Archer and Raines had brought Smith up to speed on his particular mission.

"Sir," he said, nodding. "I appreciate that."

"If every person under my command was like you, I could sleep eight hours a night."

"Begging your pardon, sir, but who *is* under your command?"

Smith glanced at his watch. "Not trying to dodge the question, Captain, but I'm afraid I don't have any more time to hang around here. The president will be broadcasting a message via closed circuit throughout the mountain and here in the resort at 1800 hours. That should answer any questions you might have."

And just like that, the cloak of secrecy was back. But Jax at least felt some satisfaction in knowing a bit more about the mystery man who shot riot cops in airports and had the ear of the top brass.

"Sir," he said, nodding.

"One more thing," said Smith. He reached under the conference table and emerged with a silver and black box. "This is for you and your men. I liberated it from the bar here at the resort."

He handed the box to Jax. It was familiar to him, though he'd never seen one outside of a locked glass case: the top featured the well-known Jack Daniels logo. Under that was the word "Monogram" and the numeral 1998.

"Sir," he breathed. "You, uh, you do realize this goes for over a thousand dollars a bottle?"

Smith grinned again. "I'll be sure to worry about that as soon as the banks reopen." He gathered up his papers. "Are you familiar with the navy rum ration, Captain?"

Jax nodded.

"Sailors were given a pint a day for their service. It was the only way they could keep men doing the shitty work of serving in the Navy during wartime. America got rid of it early on, but the British held onto the tradition until 1970. Do you know why they settled on rum?"

"Nosir."

"Because the West Indies were lousy with it. It was cheaper than fresh water." He opened the door to leave. "Seems to me we're in the same situation now, Captain. Gallons of it sitting around, waiting to be picked up. So enjoy that bottle with your men. If you develop a taste for it, I'd recommend liberating some for yourself. We might as well get some sort of compensation out of this fiasco."

Jax watched as the door swung closed behind Smith. He was still thinking about his parting words as he drove the twenty miles back to Cheyenne Mountain.

~

RUBEN LAMBERT RAISED his Styrofoam cup and the rest of the table followed suit.

"Here's to Major Smith," he said. "The mysterious, cold-ass, airport-shooting motherfucker with the excellent taste in booze."

Jax snorted a laugh out his nose, almost spilling his cup.

"Don't do that, man," he chuckled. "This stuff is expensive."

They were in the mess hall sharing the bottle with Price, who was at the mountain for medical care, along with Farries and the other five members of the Echo cavalry that had saved the day at the school. Cruz wasn't a drinker and had begged off.

Ruben leaned closer to Jax and spoke in a low voice. "So did you get any more info on Smith?"

"Naw," said Jax. "My gut's telling me he's a Virginia farm boy, hence the secrecy. Whether that's MI or INSCOM, I couldn't guess."

"Or maybe the one he works for doesn't have a name."

Jax shook his head. "Try to stay out of the rabbit holes, man. You'll get stuck down there."

Farries smacked his lips. "This stuff pretty damn good. I don't know if it's thousand-bucks-a-bottle good, but there's no denying it beats the shit I can afford on my pay."

Price was drinking with his left hand because his right was in a sling. He was lucky that the stray bullet he'd walked into at the school had only creased the flesh of his bicep.

"It's not about the quality," he said. "It's the price tag. Just like a Ferrari. Why would someone pay three hundred grand for a car that can do 200 miles an hour when the speed limit is 60? It's like paying a hooker to hold your hand. Nah, you do it so you can tell people you got so much money that you can waste three hundred grand on a car."

"Conspicuous consumption," Ruben said. "Guess that's a thing of the past now, huh?"

Jax nodded. "Another thing we have to get used to: money doesn't mean anything anymore. Which means we're going to be dealing with looters real quick."

"Then it's a good thing we sent the message we did today," said Price.

"Yeah?" Ruben looked at him. "What message would that be? That showing up with a gun you have a Constitutional right to carry will get you shot?"

"Remember who you're talking to, *Chief*," Price snapped.

"I'm just saying what a lot of civilians are going to be thinking, *sir*."

"He's right," said Jax. "The incident today isn't going to be the last one. Not by a long shot. And we need to figure out how we're going to get civilians on board with us if we're going to survive the winter."

At that moment, the screen on the wall flickered to life and Jax saw Colton Raines's face appear. He was glancing to his right at something behind the camera. Then he nodded and turned to face it, and the people watching him. Jax thought he looked like the weight of the world was on his shoulders. He supposed in a way it was.

"My fellow Americans," Raines began, then he chuckled softly. "I suppose it's a little pompous to say that these days, isn't it? The only Americans who can see this are military personnel in and around Colorado Springs. But I'm not smart enough to come up with something new, so I guess I'll keep it up."

Jax noticed Raines had the rapt attention of everyone in the room. He had a natural way of making people feel at ease that Terry Fletcher had never possessed.

"Now, my predecessors used to refer to these broadcasts as state of the union addresses, and I guess we'll keep the name, too. Traditions are important, I think, now more than ever. They help to give us a sense of stability in an unstable world, and Lord knows we have more than our fair share of instability right now.

"I'll try to be brief; I know many of you are trying to eat your supper and I don't want to keep you from it. We have some important developments that will have an effect on most of you in one way or another." He glanced down for a moment before looking back at the camera. "First and foremost, I deeply regret to inform you that Gen. Geoffrey Benton is dead."

Jax's heart let out a hard thump; judging by the looks on the faces around him, his wasn't the only one. Benton was the Chairman of the Joint Chiefs of Staff, the chief military adviser to the president, and was famous for being rock steady. Then again, so was Marcus Chase before his brain short-circuited and Jax had put four bullets in him.

"I know it's a shock, and believe me, I share your pain. Gen. Benton was one of a kind. Apparently, his vaccination wasn't enough to keep him from developing Eko. He was given one of the earlier experimental versions, and it just didn't do the job. He deserved better. Then again, I suppose millions of Americans did.

"Geoff was absolutely critical to all of you being here right now. If it hadn't been for his foresight and quick response to the outbreak, there's no way we could have established this base in time. He saw the potential disaster before anyone else, and he acted quickly and decisively. For that, this republic owes him a debt."

"Damn right," said someone in the room, to general murmurs of agreement.

"I'll get back to that in a moment. Right now, I want you to know that earlier today, I promoted Henry J. Archer to the rank of General of the Army and have named him my new chief of staff. Whenever I'm not in the room, Gen. Archer is in charge. I have every confidence in him, just as I have in his successor, Col. Robert Smith. Col. Smith will be taking over command of all of the Colorado Springs bases, as well as Cheyenne Mountain."

Ruben turned to Jax. "Looks like Smith's been promoted since he gave you that bottle. And Archer skipped straight to five-star."

"Good," Jax said. "We don't have time for politics anymore. I'm glad the president sees that."

"So we answer to Smith now? How you feel about that?"

Jax raised his cup of whiskey and shrugged. The whiskey had helped to dull the doubts that continued to nag at him—at least a little bit.

"Pretty good, right at the moment," he said, wishing he was as confident as he tried to sound.

Raines continued: "I'm sure many of you noted that I didn't use the term Chairman of the Joint Chiefs of Staff. Well, you're right. The unfortunate truth is that the military no longer has chiefs of staff."

Across from him, Jax saw Price stiffen. That probably wasn't news a marine wanted to hear.

"I'm going to be blunt here," Raines said. "The navy is no longer an entity over which I have any control, because we're a thousand miles from the nearest ocean, and we have no means of steady communication with them. And as much as I appreciate and value the members of our air force here in Colorado Springs, the very real fact remains that we won't be flying anything any time soon. What we need right now, and for the foreseeable future, is boots on the ground, ready to help our civilian population and to establish Colorado Springs as the center of the new republic."

More murmurs as that sank in. Jax had known it was coming, of course—so had Price, or at least he should have, since Archer had made it fairly clear at the meeting where they'd met.

"As of now, all military personnel are under the umbrella of the United States Army and under the command of Gen. Archer. You'll keep your ranks, obviously; you've worked hard to achieve them. We'll figure out the chain of command over the coming weeks."

Price scowled. Jax was beginning to think it was his default expression. "I guess that's that," he said.

"If you have a better idea, I'm sure the president would love to hear it," Jax sniped. "The last thing we need in this situation is more pointless politics."

"And now comes the worst part of my job," Raines sighed, running a hand through his hair. "If I'd had any idea I'd be doing something like this back when I put my name in the political ring, I would have jumped on the next plane back to Houston and taken over my daddy's shrimp boat. But I can't avoid it any longer."

Jax steeled himself for what he knew was coming.

"My friends, there are currently more than half a million people in El Paso County who are dead or dying. By the end of the week, those numbers are expected to be even higher. There's no way to sugarcoat this, so I'm just going to say it: we estimate that, when the outbreak has run its course, the population of Colorado Springs will be less than 20,000 people."

The room was silent. Jax could hear hitching breaths around him from people struggling with the news. It wasn't a surprise—it couldn't possibly have been—but that didn't ease the shock of hearing the numbers.

"I want to extend my deepest condolences to those of you who have lost loved ones to this disease, which I guess is almost all of you," said Raines, tears shimmering in his eyes. "And I want to personally thank everyone who has been working so hard at Fort Carson and Peterson and Schriever, and the folks at 21st Force Support, who have done so much to make the sick as comfortable as possible. History will never know what you've done, but *I know*, and it makes me incredibly proud. I am humbled by the sacrifices you have made for your fellow Americans."

Raines frowned and turned away from the camera for a moment. Jax found himself clearing his own throat, and he wasn't the only one. It seemed that, for the first time, they were all feeling the full weight of what was happening around them. The collapse of the United States. Hell, of the world.

"Ahem." Raines faced the camera again. "Please excuse me. As I was saying, the civilians of Colorado Springs are relying on us to help them through this crisis. And we must rely on their help, too, because we will need every single hand we can get if we're going to establish a new republic that will continue to uphold the principals that made the United States of America the greatest nation on the face of the Earth."

Before Jax realized he was doing it, his hands came together in applause. The noise seemed to spur on the men around him, who joined in. The same must have been happening wherever Raines was, because he held off on speaking for a few moments.

"I'd like to thank you all for listening to me and apologize for keeping you from your supper," he said finally. "We'll have many more of these in the days and weeks and months to come, and I'll try to time them better in the future. But before I go, I'd like to just tell you a little story that I hope will make you think.

"Back when I was a teenager, there was a major famine in Ethiopia. It was a crisis, not unlike the one we're facing, that left millions without food. Back in the U.S., a group of singers and musicians got together to record a song—maybe some of you have heard of it, it was called *We Are The World*—to raise money for relief efforts in Ethiopia and throughout Africa. It was a pretty big hit at the time.

"Now, I know what you're thinking: what the hell do a bunch of rich singers from the 1980s have to do with me, Colton? Stay with me here. This was a gathering of the biggest names in music. These folks had serious talent, and they were used to doing things their own way. But someone had the foresight to put a sign at the entrance to the studio that read: 'Check your egos at the door'.

"And, by all accounts, they did. They worked together, recorded the song and raised millions of dollars. Now, obviously, your task is infinitely more difficult than theirs, but I ask you to remember that sign. The people in charge of that recording knew that egos weren't going to feed starving people. Egos only feed themselves, and then nothing gets done.

"We are at the beginning stages of building a new republic, my friends. It will take discipline, and cooperation, and above all, it will take heart. I know you all have these qualities in spades. And I know I can count on you all to do your part, no matter how difficult the road becomes."

Raines fetched a deep sigh. "All right, I've taken up enough of your time. Thank you for listening. Good night, and God bless America."

The screen went blank. No one in the room spoke for several seconds before Ruben finally broke the silence.

"All right," he said, knocking back the last of his whiskey. "I admit it. That was actually pretty inspiring, considering the circumstances."

Jax refilled their cups and held his up in a toast.

"To President Raines."

The others lifted theirs in response and took a sip, except for Price.

"Got a problem with the president?" Jax asked.

"Pardon me if I don't toast the guy who just drafted me into the fucking army," Price groused. "And now I see what Archer was doing when he set up our little task force. I'm the token marine, Grant is the token airman and numbnuts is the token guardsman."

Jax opened his mouth to reply, but he was beaten to the punch by a voice from behind him.

"I'm sorry you see it that way, Major," Smith said as he approached the table. "Anything I can do to change your mind?"

The rest of the table stood and saluted. "Congratulations on your promotion, sir," Jax offered, but Smith ignored him.

Price was eyeing Smith warily. Smith, for his part, looked as impassive as ever, his hands clasped behind his back. “Well?” he asked.

Price waited a few beats before answering. “No sir,” he said. “Checking my ego at the door.”

Smith nodded. “Good. Now I’d appreciate it if you stopped leaving your brain at the door. Be thankful all you ended up with was that bandage after your performance at the high school today. Anything like that happens again and you’ll find yourself a private again, and I don’t think I need to tell you what kind of jobs you’ll be doing. I’m sure you’re aware that Eko victims shit themselves quite badly before they die.”

Jax looked away to avoid Price’s gaze. He hadn’t told Smith anything about the firefight, but someone obviously had. Good. Price had proved himself to be an unreliable hothead in combat, and Jax didn’t want anyone like that on his team. Even if he *was* one lucky sonofabitch.

“Yessir,” Price said. His voice was calm, but Jax swore he could hear teeth grinding.

Smith turned to Ruben and reached into his pocket. “Chief Lambert,” he said. “I’ve got something for you while I’m here.”

Ruben and Jax exchanged glances before Smith’s hand appeared and tossed two metal objects onto the table. They clanked as they landed and gleamed in the fluorescent lights. Jax recognized the pair of silver bars immediately.

“Get those on your shoulders ASAP, soldier.”

Ruben’s eyes were wide. “First lieutenant? Sir, I don’t have officer training.”

Smith looked mildly annoyed. “Lieutenant, I’ll give you this piece of advice once: don’t argue with me. You’ll always end up regretting it.”

“Yessir,” Ruben said, saluting. “Thank you, sir.”

“And give your CWO bars to Cruz the next time you see her. She’s you from now on.”

He gave them a curt salute and headed for the door. They

watched him leave in stunned silence. Once he was out the door, Jax turned to Ruben, shaking his head.

"First Louie," he said, shaking his head. "You're going to be insufferable now, aren't you?"

"I think I might have to be," Ruben breathed, staring at the bars in his hands. "For a while, anyway."

"Don't spend your raise all in one place," Price grumbled before tossing his empty Styrofoam cup on the table and stalking out of the mess hall.

The other Echoes clapped Ruben on the back and toasted his promotion. As they did, Jax saw Val Cruz enter the mess. She caught sight of their table and jogged over to his side.

"Ruben's got something for you," Jax grinned.

The look on her face told him she wasn't in a mood to celebrate.

"I need you to come with me, Captain," she said in a low voice. "It's Hayley."

14

"She's been like this since early afternoon," Val whispered. "She won't tell me what's wrong."

They were in the hallway outside the room that served as their quarters. Jax could see Hayley's back turned towards the doorway. Her back trembled softly, a sure sign she was crying.

"She didn't say anything?" he asked. He'd faced live fire earlier in the day without fear, but the thought of talking to an eight-year-old girl terrified him.

Val shook her head. "She tells me it's nothing, but it's obviously something."

"Well, if *you* can't figure it out, what hope do I have?"

"Sir, with all due respect, you're that girl's guardian. You're the only link she has to her mother. Now get the hell in there and talk to her before I kick your ass."

He gave her a sidelong look. Cruz was as tough as they came; he knew arguing with her would be pointless. The time for stalling was over.

"Make someone a chief warrant officer and suddenly they're giving orders," he muttered.

She jerked her thumb at the door; he nodded and walked toward the bunk she shared with Hayley until the girl's back was at his eye level.

"Hayley?" he said softly. "Everything okay?"

"Uh-huh." She snuffled back tears. The plastic eyes of her panda stared at him over her shoulder.

He took a deep breath. "Are you sure? You don't sound okay."

She rolled over to face him, a move he took as a win until he saw her red-rimmed eyes. It was enough to make his guts curl up in a ball. He'd seen wounded men more times than he could remember, yet the sight of this heartbroken girl stabbed him like an icepick.

"Are you scared?" he asked.

She shook her head.

"Are you sick?"

She snuffled and shook her head again, giving her bear a reflexive squeeze.

"You're going to have to give me a little more to go on, kiddo."

He glanced into the hallway to see Val leaning against the door frame, hugging herself. She was as concerned as he was, clearly. It occurred to him that he had all but dumped the girl on her since the moment they arrived at the airport in Stuttgart. Hayley wasn't Cruz's responsibility; she was his.

He turned to face the girl again. She finally met his eyes, and as she did, tears streamed out of her own and down her red cheeks.

"I can't remember her face," she husked. "I—I can't remember what she looked like."

The cramp in his heart reminded him of the moment when he'd realized that Rachel was finally gone. A bleak powerlessness that felt like a cold wind blowing through his soul. The poor kid—it had never occurred to him in all that time that she didn't have any photos of her mother.

"Oh, sweetie." Before he realized he'd done it, his hand was on her cheek. "I'm so sorry. We totally forgot to bring your phone with us when we came. And I bet your computer doesn't work anymore, does it?"

She shook her head. He reached into his pocket and pulled out his own cell, the cheap Chinese one that wouldn't hold a charge. The fates were kind enough to allow it to be working at that moment.

"Here," he said, calling up a photo of Rachel in oversized sunglasses, grinning like a Cheshire cat at an ice cream shop in downtown Boblingen. It was shortly after she'd introduced him to Hayley, and he remembered that it was the first time that he really, fully understood that she was always going to be Rachel's top priority.

And now Hayley had to be *his* top priority; he'd given Rachel his word, and if he broke a promise to the woman who had meant everything to him, then his word was worth nothing at all and he might as well have died with her.

As he showed Hayley the photo, he watched her face change, as if a light had been shone on it. The relief in her expression was almost palpable, and the tears suddenly doubled.

"Do you remember that day?" he asked.

"Yeah. My ice cream looked like spaghetti. Mom had spumoni." She glanced at him and frowned. "*You* had *vanilla*." Her tone sounded like she was accusing him of something, and he grinned in spite of himself.

"I'm a simple man," he shrugged. "You girls were always the adventurous ones."

"Can I look at more?"

"Of course. I think they're all of you and your mom anyway. There might be a few of me and Ruben, but we're not pretty like you two."

She slid her thumb across the glass surface of the phone, stopping to drink in each image. As she did, Val sidled up to the bunk.

"I bet that was kind of scary, wasn't it?" she asked. "Not remembering?"

"Uh-huh." Hayley wiped her face with her sleeve and snuffled back more snot.

"You know my mom passed away when I was a little bit younger than you."

"Yes, you told me."

"I was lucky, because back in those days, we used to print out copies of photos. That way, if your phone or your computer died, you could still look at them."

Hayley grinned. "I think I've seen those in movies."

Jax tousled her hair. "Tell you what, kid. I'll take your laptop down to Cpl. Brown and see if she can get it running. Then we'll make sure we recover all your photos, and we'll put them together with mine and print them out."

Her eyes widened. "Can we do that?"

Val nodded. "I think we can."

"That would be awesome."

"I'll get on it as soon as I can," said Jax. "Meanwhile, you can have my phone. It's kind of crappy, so you'll have to borrow somebody's charger to keep it working, but you'll be able to look at pictures of your mom whenever you want."

She looked at him. "Are you sure? Then *you* won't be able to look at them."

He felt a stab of shame as he realized he'd barely thought about Rachel since arriving at the mountain, and he certainly hadn't looked at photos. What kind of a bastard forgets about the woman he loved like that? End of the world or not, she had been *his* world for months. What kind of bastard abandons that woman's child?

"You know what, hon?" he said, biting down hard on his emotions to keep them off his face. "My memory is pretty good. But if I forget, then I might have to come here and look at them with you. Would that be okay?"

Her smile almost made him fall over. *You bastard*, he told himself. *You absolute bastard.*

"I'd like that," she said.

He leaned in close to her and returned her smile. "Me, too."

She frowned, and for a moment Jax wondered what he'd done wrong. Then she waved her free hand in front of her nose.

"Your breath smells bad, Jax," she said in a stage whisper.

"That's *booze*," said Val, grinning. "That's why I don't drink it."

"Pee-*yoo!*" Hayley giggled.

Jax feigned a look of shock. "I'm not going to sit here and be insulted," he huffed. "I will bid you ladies a good evening."

"Hit the road, Jax," said Val.

"And dontcha come back," Hayley said. "No more no more no more!"

"Take a deep breath," he said.

"Why?" she asked, but did as she was told. Jax leaned in and touched his forehead to hers.

"Good night, kiddo," he whispered. "Sleep tight."

She let out her breath. "I will. G'night."

Hayley went back to looking at photos as Val escorted Jax to the door.

"Man, when you commit, you really commit," she said.

"I did good?"

"Yeah. Now you just need to keep it up."

He nodded. "I get that now. I need you to keep me in line on this and tell me when I'm being stupid. And I need to thank you, Val. Not just for taking care of her; for... well, you know. For *everything*."

She grinned and gave his shoulders a squeeze with her powerful arm. "You get any sappier on me and you just might make me consider switching teams."

A laugh escaped Jax before he could catch it, which amazed him. Two minutes earlier he wouldn't have believed he'd ever laugh again.

"I don't honestly don't think I could handle you, Sarge."

"Damn right," she said as she walked back to her bunk. "And it's Chief now. Don't forget it, *sir*."

15

Hayley sat on the passenger side of the SUV, staring out the window as the city streets passed by them on the way to the resort HQ. For a moment, Jax thought the girl might have fallen back asleep—it was only 0700, after all—before she finally spoke.

"Are there people in those houses?" she asked quietly.

It was another hard moment in a series of them that had followed their talk in her bunk three days earlier. Jax was finding it impossible to shield Hayley from the ugly reality of their new life here in Colorado Springs, and each time he had to explain something to her, his heart cracked a tiny bit more.

"In some of them, yes," he said. "Not everyone was able to get to the hospital."

"Or the hospice, like Mom."

Jax had noticed her having an easier time talking about her mother the past few days, and he was proud of her. He himself still couldn't discuss Rachel with anyone besides Hayley, which he supposed made her braver than him.

"Some people wanted to die at home," he said. "It made them feel better."

She nodded. Jax had no idea if that was true—it could have been total bullshit for all he knew—but whatever it took to keep her from having a breakdown was worth it.

"Do you know how many kids will be at the school?" she asked.

He leapt at the chance to change the subject. The school had been announced two days earlier; Jax suspected it had been set up to keep the handful of surviving children from the bases out from underfoot. Not to mention off the overloaded minds of their parents, who were tasked with rebuilding society. Jax didn't know what was happening with civilian children yet.

"I think there are nine," he said. "Most of them have lost their parents, like you. Maybe you can all talk to each other about how it feels."

He cringed inwardly. *Dr. Booth, child psychologist.*

"Maybe," she said. "I hope we get to play games. I'm bored."

"I'm sure it'll be fun," he said. "More fun than hanging around the mountain, anyway."

"I kind of like it there. I have a lot of time to read."

He turned off of Highway 115 towards the road that led to the resort. "How are those books, anyway?"

"Good. They're about these four friends who all share the same pair of pants, and it fits all of them even though none of them are the same size."

Jack arched an eyebrow. "How does *that* work?"

She shrugged. "I dunno. You sort of have to ignore that part, I guess."

A lot like real life these days, he thought.

THE SCHOOL TURNED out to be one of the conference rooms at the hotel. The teacher was a young woman named Emily Sidley, a civilian who seemed genuinely interested in helping the kids—who ranged in age from seven up to thirteen—deal with their new circumstances. The concept of learning would have to take on a whole new meaning in the aftermath of the collapse.

Jax knelt beside Hayley before leaving her there. She'd met Ms. Sidley and nodded at a few of the other kids, and he had places to be.

"You gonna be okay?" he asked.

She nodded. "Jax?"

"Yeah, kiddo?"

"My grandparents are dead, aren't they?"

Her face was impassive, but her words hit him like a truck. He cleared his throat as he struggled to come up with an answer to a question no little girl should ever have to ask.

"It's okay if they are," she said quickly, obviously picking up on his discomfort. "I mean, I hardly even remember them."

"Honestly, Hayley, I don't know. But I won't lie—chances are very good that they got sick."

She nodded. "I kind of thought so. But I've got you, so it's okay."

Jax felt a rock roll into his throat, and he wondered how parents did it—how did they deal with these little humans constantly jabbing tiny pins into your heart? And why was he starting to crave the experience, when only a few days ago he ran from it like a cat from a junkyard dog?

Hayley wrapped her little arms around his neck and squeezed. "Have a good day. You're going to come pick me up after school?"

He hugged her back. "Nothing in the world could stop me."

She waved and walked back into the makeshift school, quickly striking up a conversation with another girl who seemed thankful for the attention. Jax smiled to himself and headed back into the hallway.

Up ahead, he could see a throng of people milling around the hotel lobby, looking serious and poring over pieces of paper. Some of Cpl. Brown's tech counterparts had managed to jury-rig a handful of computers that hadn't been connected to the Internet when the cyber weapon hit, so printing was still a thing. Jax wondered if bureaucracy would be the one thing that survived the collapse, like a metaphorical cockroach.

A flash of strawberry blond hair caught his attention: it was Lt.

Grant. It was the first time he'd seen her since they left William J. Palmer days earlier, which already felt like a month ago. She glanced up as he approached and, recognizing him, saluted.

"Sir," she said.

"Lieutenant. How's life in the resort?"

She gave him a half-smile. "Living the dream."

"Just remember you're talking to a guy who bunks in a closet in a hole under a mountain."

"At least you're not flushing your toilet and washing yourself with bottled water."

She had him there. The mountain had its own self-contained everything. The hotel, like the city, was on water rationing and dealing with rolling brownouts. No one seemed to know how long the water supply could last without staff to man the treatment plant; no one would die of thirst, but personal hygiene was taking a major hit. For some reason, it reminded Jax of a quote by Frank Sinatra, who'd been his dad's favorite singer; whenever a waiter would bring Sinatra a glass of water, he'd say: "I'm thirsty, not dirty. Bring me a bourbon."

Electricity wasn't quite as pressing an issue, given the supply of gas and generators, but the city's coal-fired power plant would soon stop operating for good. And heat would be foremost in everyone's mind in a couple of months as winter settled into the Rockies.

It occurred to Jax that a significant amount of the paperwork he'd made fun of a few minutes earlier was probably focused on things like that, and he felt a twinge of shame. Everyone had a job to do these days.

"I see you got some army fatigues," he said. "So you've drank the Kool Aid?"

She shrugged, but Jax could read sourness in her face. "I didn't see a choice, so I figured go along to get along. Checking my ego at the door and all that."

"How's Col. Roth handling it?"

She glanced around the room before leaning in closer.

"I haven't seen him since the president's broadcast," she said in a low voice. "I honestly don't know where he is or what he's doing."

"Holed up somewhere pouting, maybe?" Jax asked. The thought of a senior leader like Nicholas Roth sucking his thumb over who ran what was repellent to him.

Carly shook her head. "I know it seems like that, but that's not the way he is. He wouldn't have gotten his command if he was like that."

Jax wondered. He liked to think the military didn't promote certain types of people, but he also didn't fool himself into believing it was always like that.

"Speaking of commanders," she said. "Looks like we have a new one. Anything you can tell me about Col. Smith?"

There's a lot I could tell you, he thought but didn't say.

"We think he may be former intelligence," he said. "As no-nonsense as they come. He gave me a bottle of primo whiskey as a reward for our outing at the high school. Sorry, I didn't think to save you any."

She smiled. "I'm a beer gal. Which means I better get used to drinking it warm, at least until winter gets here. So... we weren't put on report for taking out civilians?"

"The opposite, actually." He shook his head. "Col. Archer—sorry, Gen. Archer—was the same way on this. The president wants us to extend an olive branch, but Archer and Smith say to keep a loaded weapon in the other hand."

Her face betrayed a sudden desperation. "I'm a pencil pusher," she said. "I've never been in combat. Never fired my weapon outside of the range. This is all beyond me. I shouldn't be on your team."

Jax put a hand on her arm. "I think that's exactly why you *are* on the team. The last thing we need is a bunch of testosterone factories running into situations shooting first and asking questions later. Don't sell yourself short, Carly. I need you on this."

"Really?" The relief in her voice was palpable. "Thank you, sir, I appreciate that."

He nodded. "I think we can belay the 'sirs' from now on. The chain of command isn't going to snap if we start using each other's first names."

"All right," she smiled. "Jackson, right?"

"Call me Jax."

They stood in silence for a moment. Jax felt like he'd taken a step forward somehow. He wasn't exactly sure what it meant, but it felt right.

"Jax," she said. "Can I ask you something?"

"Of course."

The look in her eyes was oddly fragile. "The incident at the high school… was that just the beginning of what's to come?"

He wished to God he knew the answer to that one.

"I honestly don't know," he said. "I hope it wasn't, but we have to think like it was."

She nodded. "It's a whole new world out there."

"It is," he said. "But I think we have to start thinking of it in the president's terms. For us, here, now, it's a whole new republic."

16

Anna Mathis was supposed to be at soccer practice.

It was Thursday, and Thursday was her day to bring orange slices to Ryan's team at the middle school. They were only eight, but they had to play at the middle school field because of scheduling. Anna didn't do the scheduling, she did the orange slices. Every Thursday.

She glanced at the watch on her wrist. Unlike her phone, the watch still worked. The time was 3:30 p.m. She felt a pang of panic—she still didn't have any oranges, and practice was about to start. And she was still almost a mile from the school.

The Safeways all seemed to be closed, so she was hurrying to the Save-A-Lot that she'd been boycotting ever since the bag boy had made eyes at her last summer. She supposed she could put up with it if it meant she could get her bag of oranges. She wouldn't have time to slice them; she hoped that would be okay. Sure it would. She could peel them and pull them into segments. That would be okay. That would be fine.

She noticed the cigarette in her hand as it pulled away from her mouth, and suddenly remembered that she had started smoking again. She shook her head; nine years down the tubes. She'd quit the day she learned she was pregnant with Ryan and hadn't had a puff since, until—until when? When had she started again?

She pushed the thought away as she scurried up the street. Didn't matter when. She was smoking again, that was that.

Up ahead, she saw the bright red and blue letters of the Save-A-Lot sign. The front door underneath was open: she would get her oranges. Her relief felt as good as a glass of cool water in the afternoon heat.

She pitched her cigarette onto the ground as she approached the door. It vaguely occurred to her that the parking lot was empty. All that meant was more oranges for her.

Inside, Anna saw that the lights were out. There had been rolling brownouts forever, it seemed, so it wasn't a surprise. She walked through the door, ignoring the fact that there was no one manning the tills next to the entrance. No bag boys to ogle her today.

She steadfastly ignored the smell that assailed her nostrils.

Produce was off to the right, so she made her way past the aisles of processed foods: snacks and potato chips and bulk peanuts. She didn't let Ryan touch any of that stuff. Fresh fruits and vegetables were what growing boys needed. Everybody knew that.

Ignoring the smell got harder as she got closer to the produce section; it got worse with each step, and with each step she felt panic rise a little higher in her chest. Why did the smell affect her like this? She needed to go to the doctor.

No doctor! her mind screamed at her. *No doctor, never again!*

Anna realized she was hugging herself as she caught sight of the fruit section. This wasn't right—the bins were empty. The ones that weren't had a few mouldering pieces slowly liquefying inside them. She saw shapes that had once been round and orange but were now powdery blue and looked like deflated balls.

"Oranges," she heard herself whisper.

"There's no oranges here, lady."

The sound from behind her almost made her jump out of her skin. She spun around to see an elderly man in a mechanic's coveralls. He was carrying a fabric tote filled with cans.

"The fruit's all rotten," the man said. "Can'tcha see that?"

"My son's practice," she rasped, and the sound of her own voice was strange in her ears. When had she last spoken? "I need—I need orange slices..."

He frowned at her. "There's no practices anymore, lady. There's no *anything* anymore."

As he said the words, Anna finally tuned into the sounds that she had been ignoring since she came in on her quest for oranges. White noise in her ears. People nattering. *Natter natter natter.*

"I guess," she said, then stopped for a moment. "I guess they'll just have to go without. Just for today. They'll be thirsty, though."

As she said it, she realized she herself was monstrously thirsty.

The old man was shaking his head now. "I don't know what you're on, lady, but if I was you, I'd grab what I could carry and get the hell outta here. That's what everybody else is doing."

Everybody? Now that she was letting the voices in, she was also registering movement. People pushing shopping carts filled with cans of food, bottles of water and soda. A lot of them looked like they hadn't showered in days.

When was the last time I *showered?*

Just as the thought struck her, she caught the reflection of a face in the chrome strapping around the upright produce stand next to her. Who was she looking at? Those sunken eyes, the sallow cheeks. That woman needed a meal, fast. She was wasting away.

Anna refused to believe it was her own reflection, just as she refused to believe that she'd watched Ryan die in his bed at Fort Carson four days earlier. She refused to believe that she'd found her husband, Garry, in a pool of his own blood on the living room floor of their little downtown condo, the shotgun he used for duck hunting lying askew next to him.

There were no oranges here. She looked at the old man and shook her head.

"I really hate having to go to Walmart," she said. "But I need oranges, so I guess I don't have any choice. Have a nice day."

As she walked past him toward the entrance, she heard him

mutter something that sounded like *grazing bits.* She didn't need any grazing bits, she needed oranges. And she would keep going until she found them.

She absently lit another cigarette as she left the darkness of the Save-A-Lot and walked into the bright sunshine of the afternoon.

17

"They shot him in the back," the long-haired kid said, scowling. "They shot him in the fucking back and nobody has said boo to me about it, let alone apologized."

Rob Taylor nodded. The people around him nodded. They'd all heard the stories out of William J. Palmer. The army had invited people to a meeting and it ended with a dozen people shot dead. As if there weren't enough dead people around already. Rob's own parents were dead out at Fort Carson. The only way he'd found out was by reading a notice that the army had posted on bulletin boards around the city.

"It's an attack on our rights," said a man who'd introduced himself as Steve when Rob had met him earlier. "We're American fucking citizens and we have rights."

They and a group of about twenty others had been hanging around the playground of a downtown park for the last few hours, drinking from a half-dozen cases of warm Coors they'd taken from an abandoned 7-11 up the street. Most of them were men, ranging in age from late teens to late sixties. A handful of women had joined them, though none of them were of an age that Rob would have been looking for in a date.

He kicked back the rest of his beer and tossed the can into a pile next to the slide, thinking vaguely about his mom. His old man had been an asshole, no loss there, but his mom was nice to him. Made him spaghetti when he'd asked for it.

He'd been living in an abandoned condo a few blocks from the park for the last several days. His parents' home, the house he grew up in, was fine but it wasn't close to things, and driving was next to impossible these days. So he'd moved downtown to be close to places where he could steal supplies.

"That's just it," said a middle-aged guy with thinning hair and a button-down shirt. "Rights can be suspended. Might makes right, and the army has the might. Nothing we can do about it."

A murmur of agreement ran through the group. Another older guy said: "Yeah, but some of *them* are dying from the disease, too. And from what I can see, their technology is just as fucked as ours. Their electric vehicles still seem to work, but they're using analog radios."

More agreement from the group, interspersed with the hissing crack of beer cans being opened. The long-haired kid reached down to the bench next to him and patted the stock of a military-style rifle, the kind Rob had seen in war movies. There was a gym bag full of ammunition clips next to it.

"This is all the technology I need," the kid said, then followed it with a mammoth belch. Rob was pretty sure the guy wasn't old enough to legally drink, but what the hell did that matter anymore?

"And what are you going to do with it?" asked a middle-aged woman in a gray track suit. Fashion didn't seem to be on anyone's mind these days. "Take on the army? Look where that got your father."

"Don't talk about my dad," the kid warned. Rob didn't like the look in his eyes.

"And don't talk to ladies that way," said the man in the button-down shirt.

"I'll fucking do what I want."

The mood was starting to kill Rob's buzz, so he pulled another Coors from the case next to him.

"All I know is that our rights are being trampled," said Steve. His ass was propped against a cedar post. "And we aren't even getting anything in return from them."

"That's not true," said the lady in the track suit. "The army took care of my Frank until—until the end. They let me stay at Fort Carson with him."

"And then what?" Steve asked. "What did they do after he died?"

She frowned. "They brought me back here."

"And abandoned you."

"They've been bringing water and canned food—"

"Wow, aren't they heroes? Sounds more like a pet owner to me."

"Look," said the man in the button-down shirt. "I just don't know what else we *can* do. I'm a financial advisor—*was* a financial advisor. What am I going to do to help people? Tell them to liquidate their retirement assets?"

Rob was growing tired of the conversation. The last few days, he'd found himself growing tired of everything: the boredom, the canned food, the loneliness. He finished his beer and cracked another.

"I know what *I'm* gonna do," said the long-haired kid. "I'm gonna fight back."

"Yeah?" Steve asked, clearly intrigued. "How are you going to do that?"

"My dad had a lot of guns. Anyone who wants one can have one. We can take back this city."

"Whoa," said the older guy. "Let's not start talking like that."

"Why not?" asked a guy in his thirties who'd been silent until now. "My wife and kids are dead. What did the fucking government do to stop that? Nothing, that's what. There's a lot more of those soldiers alive than the rest of us, seems to me."

"You don't know that," said the middle-aged woman. "There are so many sick and dying—"

"Not everybody's dying," said Steve. "I met a guy who said he got sick but then he got better. He's still pretty messed up, but he's alive. Weirdest thing is his eyes are two different colors now. Freaky as hell."

"See?" The long-haired kid pitched his empty Coors can and lit a cigarette. More people seemed to be smoking now that coffin nails were free, Rob noted. "They got a cure, they're just not giving it to us. They're keeping it for themselves."

More murmurs through the crowd. As they talked, Rob looked at the kid's gun. It looked powerful. He wondered how it would feel in his hands, how heavy it would be. What kind of a kick it would have.

"I'm not going to have anything to do with this," said the middle-aged woman, walking away. A number of other women joined her, as did some of the men.

But there were plenty who didn't walk away, Rob noticed. He was one of them.

"You guys are smart," said the kid. "You see that something's gotta be done."

"Where's your house?" Steve asked.

A slow, greasy smile spread across the kid's face. "Follow me, gentlemen. This is how movements start. People don't recognize 'em right away, but they read about them in the history books."

Rob grabbed another can of Coors as the crowd began to mobilize, the long-haired kid in the lead. As he cracked his beer, he wondered what it would be like to be written up in a history book.

18

It was the first time Jax had heard an alarm go off since he'd arrived at Cheyenne Mountain. The jangling put his teeth on edge as he headed for the designated muster point in the mess hall.

The sound stopped after about thirty seconds, which Jax was grateful for. The rest of Echo Company was streaming into the mess alongside him, all of them in combat gear, like Jax. He didn't want to think about what the emergency might be, and found himself hoping it was just a drill.

It wasn't. Col. Smith stood placidly at the front of the room next to the kitchen, his hands behind his back, as the rest lined up along the walls. While they were taking their places, Ruben jogged up next to Jax.

"Drill?" he asked hopefully.

"Look at Smith," Jax said. "Now ask again."

"Shit."

Jax approached his CO. "Sir. What's going on?"

"Rioting in the Springs." As usual, Smith sounded like he was talking about a drywall delivery. "Armed, at least twenty of them, attacking downtown stores. Guns and Molotov cocktails. You need to get it under control."

"Yessir."

Smith leaned in. "Downtown is a critical area for supplies," he said. "Keep them secure at all costs."

Jax arched an eyebrow. "Can you clarify that, sir?"

"I'm telling you to deal with this the same way you did with the people at the high school. Extreme prejudice."

"Is there anyone in harm's way?"

"There are supplies being burned," Smith said, mild annoyance creeping into his voice. "We can't make more. Do whatever is necessary to secure them. That's an order."

Jax took a deep breath. "Yessir." He turned to face his men. "A and B Groups, this is yours. Get to the motor pool and secure a transport. We'll need a bullhorn. Lt. Lambert and I will follow in an SUV. The rest of you fall out."

"Two groups," Ruben said as he sidled up to Jax. "Is thirty men enough for this?"

"Thirty highly trained counter-terrorist specialists against a dozen armed civilians? I think so."

"What was Smith saying?"

Jax thought for a moment before lying: "He told me to do whatever it takes to keep from having another Palmer High on our hands."

It was the first time in his career that he'd countermanded an order. Something told him it wasn't going to be the last.

THE TRANSPORT TRUCK stopped two blocks from the center of downtown and dropped off the members of Echo Company. Jax and Ruben pulled up next to them, the electric SUV's motor thrumming.

Jax pulled the portable bullhorn from the backseat and gave the button a few test squelches. Loud and clear.

"Ready when you are, sir," Farries said from behind him. The men stood at ease, rifles tilted downwards towards the street.

Another SUV pulled up alongside them. Three people in combat gear got out: Jax recognized them as Grant, Price and Skolnik. The guardsman looked like he was dressed in an ill-fitting Halloween costume.

"Sir," Grant said. "Reporting as ordered."

"What are these two doing here?" Price asked. "They don't have combat experience."

"Neither did any of the men behind you until the first time," said Jax. "Everyone has to lose their cherry sometime, especially these days. And since you're so battle-hardened, Major, you can take up position with the Echoes."

Price scowled but did as he was told. As he did, Jax leaned in to Carly and Skolnik.

"Stay low and stay back," he said. "Draw your weapons only as a last resort. Clear?"

The two nodded. Jax took his position at the front of the group, Ruben at his side.

"Archer would kill you if he saw you in front," said Ruben.

"Yeah, well, Archer's a bureaucrat now."

With that, Jax motioned for them to move forward toward the smoke that was billowing upward two blocks away.

JAX NOTED with relief that the fire was contained to a strip mall that was surrounded by concrete. There was almost no chance of it spreading, which was good, because he had no idea if water would still come out of the city's hydrants, assuming there was anyone around to man the city's pumper trucks. Given the fact there weren't any on scene, he was pretty sure he knew the answer.

Even without the smoke, they need only have followed the sound of gunfire to find the rioters. As Jax had suspected, most of the twenty or so men were firing their weapons at the walls of buildings and laughing as chunks of brick and concrete sprayed all over the street.

"Those men are hammered," Ruben said from his flank.

"They are," said Jax. "Which means our job could be easy or it could be hard." He turned to his men. "No one fires without my order!"

Before he could take another step, he heard a screeching noise as a vehicle rounded a corner next to the strip mall. By the time Jax had registered the El Paso County Sheriff logo on the door, Maggie Stubbs had jammed the car into park and leapt out the driver's side door.

Beside him, Ruben chuckled. "The woman's got guts, man."

"Yeah," Jax grumbled. "Too bad she doesn't have brains."

As they advanced, he could hear the sheriff trying to be heard over the gunfire and the men's shouts. Most of them were focused on the buildings in front of them; one, a kid with long hair, was in the process of stuffing a rag into the mouth of a red jerry can.

Maggie turned to see Echo Company and her head dropped back. Jax couldn't hear her, but he knew she was letting out an exasperated groan. She turned and jogged toward him, leaving the rioters, who still hadn't noticed any of them, behind her.

"Sheriff," Jax grinned. "Fancy meeting you here."

"I know how this looks," she said. "But these guys are just drunk idiots letting off steam."

"They're endangering vital supplies."

She shook her head in frustration. "Supplies of what? It's an accounting office, a lingerie shop and pizza place. I think we can get by without them, don't you?"

"If you're worried that there's going to be a repeat of the high school, don't be," Jax said. "Unless they force our hands again."

"We just need to talk to them!" she cried. "They'll listen to reason, especially after what happened at the school!"

Jax pulled the bullhorn from its place strapped to his shoulder and handed it to her.

"Just hit that button with your thumb."

She looked at him sidelong. "You're going to let *me* do this?"

"We have to start working together some time," he said. "Consider us backup. For now."

She took the bullhorn as if she still didn't believe him, then turned to face the crowd. Jax grabbed her shoulder and pulled him to her.

"You might want to do that from a position of cover," he said sternly. "Unless you want to startle a bunch of drunk idiots with semi-automatic weapons."

She blinked at him for a few seconds before nodding. Jax motioned for everyone to move into the alley behind an apartment building. He was amazed that none of the men had noticed them yet, which reinforced the belief that they weren't really dangerous.

Jax waved Ruben, Carly, Price and Maggie to his side at the corner of the building where the alley met the street.

"All right," he said. "Once you get their attention, all of us will walk out into the street."

Grant and Skolnik exchanged startled glances, but the rest of them nodded.

"Showtime," Maggie said, bringing the bullhorn to her lips.

"ATTENTION!" The volume was deafening and the feedback whine was like a drill in Jax's ears, but it worked. The gunfire stopped immediately.

"This is Sheriff Maggie Stubbs!" the horn blared. "I order you to lay down your weapons and leave the area immediately!"

From his position, Jax could see a group of the men noticing Maggie's cruiser for the first time. Several of them were swaying noticeably.

"Fuck you!" one of them yelled.

"Give them the last call speech," Jax said.

Maggie clicked the button again, clearly nervous. "If you drop your guns and walk away, we won't pursue you. No other action will be taken. If you don't, you will be taken into custody by any means necessary, including deadly force. You have two minutes to comply."

Jax nodded as she lowered the horn. "Not bad."

"This isn't my first rodeo," she said with a frown. "I did learn something from Palmer High, you know."

"So did I. Which is why I let you have the horn."

"Hey!" one of the rioters shouted. "There's soldiers in the alley!"

"Fuck that!" another cried, and Jax heard a loud *clack* as a rifle hit the asphalt. "I'm outta here!"

A chorus of *clacks* as more weapons struck the pavement. People talking over top of each other, voices fading into the distance.

Jax took the opportunity to lean his head around the corner. Five men were left: two were still armed, two were motioning frantically with their hands as they argued with the others. He noticed the kid with the long hair was still holding his makeshift firebomb in one hand and a lighter in the other.

"Cover me," he said, stepping forward.

"No!" Maggie stopped him with an arm across his chest. "Let me finish this."

Jax saw the look in her eyes and considered for a few moments before finally nodding. He had always trusted his instincts in combat, and he was learning to do the same in this new, volatile arena. And his gut was telling him to let her do her thing.

Maggie turned the corner into the street. Behind Jax, two members of Echo took up position behind a green garbage bin, rifles pointed at the remaining holdouts from the riot. Behind them, flames continued to pour out of the blackened shell of the strip mall, sending plumes of acrid smoke into the sky.

The sheriff raised her hands and approached the men slowly. "I'm serious, gentlemen," she said. "There are some very unhappy soldiers in that alley. Now, I can probably get them to calm down, but not if you don't all get out of here immediately."

The two remaining armed men dropped their weapons, to the obvious relief of the other two. The long-haired kid still held his jerry can, a cold stare leveled at the alley.

"You're not gonna come after us?" one of the men asked. He looked like a kid who'd been caught filching a cookie from the jar and couldn't quite believe he wasn't in trouble.

"No," Maggie said. "But I'm going to remember your faces. This is a one-time deal, gentlemen. If you try it again, my friends in the alley will be the ones who deal with you, and they are nowhere near as forgiving as I am."

Jax smiled. Good cop, bad cop. A simple strategy, but it seemed to be working. He wondered if it might not have prevented a tragedy if they'd used it at the school.

"This isn't over," one of the men slurred as they turned to make their way east from the burning building. "We got rights. You can't just take over."

"Shut up," another hissed, pulling him along. They almost tripped over their own feet as they retreated.

That left Long Hair and his jerry can. He was still glaring at Jax.

"What about you, chuckles?" Maggie asked. "You think we're bluffing, then you don't know what happened a few days ago at Palmer High."

"Oh, I know about it," the kid said quietly.

"Then you know what happens if you don't drop that can."

The kid stood there for a full thirty seconds, until Jax was almost certain he would have to order one of the snipers behind the garbage bin to shoot the can out of his hand.

Finally, the kid leaned down and put the can on the ground. His eyes never left the alley.

"No problem here," he said to Maggie as he stood up. "Sorry for the trouble, Sheriff. It was stupid of us to go after this place. Won't happen again."

He kept his gaze on the alley as he turned to walk away. Finally, he started looking where he was going and kept on in that direction. Maggie kept her eyes on him until he disappeared a block later.

Jax left the alley and joined her in the street, Ruben at his side. Carly, Price and Skolnik followed.

"Looks like we're getting better at this," Ruben said.

Skolnik's eyes were wide. "I don't believe it. I thought for sure I was going to die."

"Jesus," Price grumbled.

"Nice work," Jax said to Maggie.

"Thanks. And thanks for giving me the option."

He thought for a moment, then said: "Are you—attached? I mean, do you have anyone at home?"

Her cheeks flushed, and suddenly Jax realized what he'd just said.

"I didn't mean—it's just that, if you don't have anyone to, you know, go home to, you could join us."

She looked even more stunned. "I—I don't know if I can do that."

"Things are just going to get worse out here. Cheyenne Mountain has running water, power, heat. The resort isn't quite as self-sufficient, but it's better than out here."

She bit her lip. "Can I think about it?"

Jax nodded. "Chances are you're going to end up drafted anyway," he said. "Might as well beat the rush."

He gave her a radio and showed her how to use it to contact him at Cheyenne.

"Drafted," she said quietly. "Yeah. I guess I have to think about that."

IN AN ALLEY TWO BLOCKS AWAY, Malcolm Austin stopped and propped an arm against a ramshackle fence that barely held his weight. He pulled out his member and urinated on the crabgrass that had taken over the fence line where it met the gravel.

"Stupid to go after that place," he muttered to himself. His long hair draped down over his face as he leaned against the fence. "Want to get somethin' done, we need to go after *people*."

He gave himself a shake and zipped up his jeans before shuffling back into the late afternoon heat.

19

"Your liberating skills aren't up to Smith's," Ruben said as he glanced at the brown liquid in the cup.

Jax shrugged. "I had to go with what was at hand. Unfortunately, 7-11 isn't known for its selection of top-shelf whiskey."

He'd stopped the transport on their way back to Cheyenne and given the men orders to grab whatever they wanted. The food had been pretty much picked through—convenience stores were the hardest hit by looting, since the majority of their wares were so highly processed they'd still be good years from now—but there was still lots of booze left. It just wasn't quite up to the level they'd reached with their last bottle.

Now they were in the mess, celebrating the fact that no one had been killed that afternoon. A report from a routine patrol said the fire was close to burning itself out. Subsequent patrols would monitor it overnight.

Ruben took a swig and grimaced. "Smooth," he gasped.

"Yeah, yeah." Jax knocked back some of his own and found himself slapping the table. He swallowed hard. "Okay, point taken."

It was the first time Jax could remember feeling relaxed since they'd arrived at Cheyenne. He didn't know if he was building up a spiritual callous to the situation, or if it was just the satisfaction of a successful mission, but he was actually in a good mood.

"How was Hayley's first day of school?" Ruben asked.

"I don't know if you'd call it school, exactly," Jax said. He noticed Ruben was sipping a little more easily now. "But I think it was good for her. She said they spent the day playing games. The older kids were the leaders."

"That's better than nothing, I guess."

"The teacher said her orders are to keep the kids occupied, and to answer their questions honestly. That's about all we can expect right now."

Ruben refilled his cup. Apparently he was as eager to drink as Jax.

"How are things with you and Hayley?"

Jax nodded. "Better, I think. You know me, man. I don't know what I'm doing with all this. I'm used to shouting orders, not talking to kids."

"Nobody knows what they're doing at first. You learn as you go." He drank. "Not that I know any more than you do."

"I guess. We hung out for a while after school, just shooting the breeze. Had supper together."

Ruben grinned and raised his cup. "All right! That's something, man."

Beside Jax, three other Echoes who had been drinking together suddenly lurched to their feet and saluted. He glanced to his left and saw Archer walking toward their table just as Ruben did. The two of them followed suit even more awkwardly.

"At ease," the general barked. "Jesus, men, don't put yourself in a cast just to salute me. We need every able body we can get."

They sat back down and Archer took the seat next to Jax. He nodded at Ruben across the table.

"Congratulations on your promotion, Lieutenant," he said. "Well deserved."

"Thank you, sir, I appreciate it. Same to you."

"They couldn't have picked a better man for the job, sir," said Jax.

"All right, holster those lips, my ass is chapped enough as it is."

Archer picked the bottle off the table and scowled. "Where do you men shop for whiskey, 7-11? You know this stuff is just lying around, right?"

They glanced at each other, embarrassed.

"I don't have much time," he said. "This fucking job is going to kill me. I just wanted you to know I read your report, Captain. Nice work out there today. I don't know if I would have had the patience for that kind of reaction myself."

Jax nodded. "Sir. I'm just glad we're making some progress."

Archer leaned in. "What are your first impressions of Smith?"

Jax chose his words carefully. He knew Archer valued his opinion, but he also had to keep working for Smith.

"The colonel doesn't mince words," he said. "That's a plus in our situation, I think."

"Mm. I was hoping you'd say that. He—well, I'll just say he comes highly recommended."

Ruben nodded. "What's his background, sir? if you don't mind me asking?"

Jax glared at him. *Subtle*, that look said. Ruben ignored him.

"Classified," said Archer. "I know that's not what you want to hear." He sighed. "Everything in this new job is classified, it seems."

Jax thought the general's expression was oddly nervous, which wasn't something he associated with the old man. Then again, these days everyone seemed to be experiencing a whole gamut of new emotions, himself included.

"Anyway, Smith knows what he's doing," the general said. "Follow his orders just as you always followed mine."

That made Jax wonder what Smith thought of his actions that afternoon. His orders had almost sounded like he was telling Jax to go in and mow down the protestors, but he could have been wrong. The fact that he handled it another way hadn't resulted in any official rebuke from Smith—yet.

Archer rose. "All right, I need to get a move on. Meeting the president at HQ."

"Sir, before you go," Jax said. "I had occasion today to consider drafting the acting sheriff of El Paso County into our little unit. She's been an asset to us twice."

He nodded. "I read the report. We can use every good soldier we can get. Run it past Smith first, but make it happen."

"Sir."

Archer gave a cursory salute and marched out before the rest of Echo even realized he was gone. Ruben poured himself another shot of whiskey, then topped up Jax's cup.

"What do you think he meant by 'everything is classified'?"

Jax shrugged. "Why do you ask?"

"Seems to me there's no point in classifying anything anymore. I mean, what's worse than what we already know? You can't hide what's going on from anyone. It's as in-your-face as you can get."

"I suppose they need to keep their plans quiet. There are some tough decisions ahead, especially with winter coming. A lot of sacrifices that'll have to be made. And we still don't know how the whole relationship with civilians is going to roll out."

Ruben sighed. "Yeah, all right, I hear you. I just can't help thinking about this old song that keeps going through my head. Remember those Jason Bourne movies when we were kids?"

"Yeah. Could sure use a guy like him right about now."

"Ain't that the truth. Anyway, that song that used to play at the end credits?"

Jax nodded. "Yeah, something with a synthesizer. I remember."

"It's called *Extreme Ways*. There's a line in it about so many dirty things you couldn't even believe. I can't get it out of my head."

Jax finished his whiskey and poured more. He was starting to feel a warm blanket wrapping around his brain, dulling the sharp edges that his thoughts seemed to sport these days.

"How about we stop talking about this?" he said. "You're killing my buzz."

Ruben tipped back his own cup and emptied it. "I'm on board with that. I'm killing my *own* damn buzz."

By the time they both stumbled back to their bunks later that night, they'd finished that bottle and half of another.

20

Malcolm Austin had realized his fatal mistake, and he was telling everyone in the park who would listen.

The area had become a gathering place in the wake of the ill-fated attack on the strip mall two days earlier. A lot of people from outlying areas, like Rob Taylor, had gravitated downtown to spend their days commiserating with other survivors and scavenging for whatever they could find.

"We shouldn't have done it drunk," Austin told a group that included Rob, Steve, and a couple of others who had turned tail when the sheriff offered them amnesty that afternoon. Others around them talked among themselves; several of them were drinking.

"No shit," said Steve. "That was the first mistake. The other was not knowing what the fuck we were doing."

Rob nodded, vaguely agreeing. He wasn't sure why he'd bothered to get involved that day, but part of it was definitely the beer. Another factor was that it was something to do, and firing off some rounds was wicked fun.

Austin shook his head. "I knew what I was doing," he said. "I was protesting. I was demonstrating that we got rights."

"Yeah, and what did it get us?" Steve asked. "Nothing, that's what. We're lucky we didn't get shot like your old man."

"That's another thing we're doing," Austin said, pointing a finger at his companion. "We're fucking protesting that they killed my dad."

"I want to protest that we don't have any electricity!" Rob interjected, suddenly angry. "I'm sick of using that camp lantern. And using bottled water to wash my hands."

A few people around them who had been silent started nodding.

"He's right," said Steve. "I can't even take a shower. I reek, man."

Rob nodded. He'd moved to a motel nearby because the smell in the condo he had been staying in got to be too much. There must have been people who died in the other units. He chose his new quarters based on the belief that nobody went to a motel to die. A few others here in the park had followed his lead and were now his neighbors.

"I met a woman in another suite who looks like she hadn't eaten in a week," he said. "I think she's kind of gone soft in the head, too. All she does is sit there chain-smoking and asking me if I know where to get oranges. She needs help."

Nods and agreement all around. "Lots of people like that," someone in the crowd said.

"That's why we need to make a plan," Austin said loudly. "So let's do it!"

"Okay," said Rob. "You go first, seeing as how you're so smart."

More murmurs of agreement. Apparently Rob wasn't the only one who was tired of the guy's constant nattering. Either do something or shut up about it.

Malcolm shot him a defiant look. "All right, I say we go right into that base at Cheyenne Mountain and storm the place. They've got a huge supply of fresh water, and a power plant. I bet there's a shitload of food in there, too."

The comment elicited stunned silence from the group for a handful of seconds. Then they broke into peals of laughter.

"Are you out of your fucking mind?" Steve hooted. "I went on a field trip to that place when I was in junior high. The front door is, like, three feet thick. And it's full of soldiers, you moron! Yeah, we got guns, but they've got better ones, and they're trained!"

Rob shook his head. "Are you even from here, dude?"

A sullen scowl was Austin's only reply.

"We need to face facts," said Steve. "We have to do what the army tells us. Either that or head into the woods to live, and I'm not ready to do that. It's gonna get Christly cold here in a couple of months, and I don't feel like living in a tent and eating rabbit over an open fire all winter."

"You'd rather live here as a slave, then?" said a man behind Rob. He turned to see a guy who looked to be in his late forties who'd been hanging around at the back of the group for the past several hours. Rob thought he'd seen him around a couple times in the past few days, too. He always wore plain T-shirts that showed off his muscular frame, and his close-cropped hair was starting to creep toward silver.

"What are you talking about?" Steve asked. "I'm not anybody's slave, man. Forget that shit right now."

"That's what they want you to be," the man said, stepping forward. As he did, Rob noticed a pair of military issue boots on the guy's feet. "They need slaves, and you people are it."

"That's crazy," Steve scoffed. "Paranoia. We have rights. It's in the Constitution. We just need to fight for them."

"With rifles?" the man asked. "Jerry cans full of gasoline? How'd that work out for you the last time?"

Malcolm Austin finally rejoined the conversation. "It's more than you did," he said. "You weren't even there."

"I was watching from a distance. Didn't want to be caught up when the army decided to crack down on you, which I knew they would."

"Fuck you, man," Austin grumbled. "Least we did *something*."

"I'm all for doing something," said the man. "I just prefer to do it right. Have a plan. Be prepared. Hit them where it hurts."

Austin seemed to perk up at that; this guy was speaking his language. Rob himself was curious now, too.

"What're you talking about?" Rob asked.

"If you want to have a real effect, you're going to need a real plan. One that can maximize your strengths and exploit your enemy's weaknesses. Then you need *real* weapons, ones that can match those that you'll be going up against."

"Like what?" Steve asked, clearly intrigued.

"Rocket launchers, .50-caliber machine guns, grenades. That kind of thing."

Austin scoffed. "Yeah, okay," he said. "We'll just head over to Walmart and grab that shit, then we'll come back here and you can make your plan."

A chuckle ran through the crowd. The man waited patiently for it to die down before he continued.

"We'll make the plan first," he said. "As for the weapons, I know where to get my hands on everything we need. I just need your help."

Rob's eyes narrowed. "Who the hell are you, anyway?"

The man offered his outstretched hand. "My name is Nick Roth. Pleased to meet you."

21

"So if I sign up, do I get to live here?" Maggie asked as they took their seats at the conference table.

Carly Grant shook her head. "The hotel's not as great as you might think."

"It beats my shitty apartment. At the very least, the beds have got to be better than my futon."

"You do know you can pretty much move in anywhere in the city," Jax said, taking his own seat opposite Maggie and beside Carly. "Squatters' rights."

"Yeah," said Ruben. "Except for, you know—*previous tenants*, if you get my drift."

"We get it," Jax said with a sarcastic grin. "Thanks for the image."

Carly and Maggie both tried to hide a giggle and couldn't. Maybe there was hope for this thing yet.

"Moving along," Jax said. "We're just waiting on a couple of folks from logistics. Then we can get down to business."

As if on cue, the door opened and a middle-aged woman hobbled into the room, followed closely by a young Asian man with a clipboard.

"Pardon our tardiness," said the woman. "It's not easy to get around this place on a bad hip. I'm Capt. Jill Beckett, this is Lt. Carey Fujita."

Jax made the rest of the introductions as the new arrivals took their seats.

"Sorry to hear about your hip," he said to Beckett. "That must be rough for you in these new circumstances."

She smiled. "I like that. 'New circumstances'. You should be in politics."

If you only knew, he thought morosely.

"Don't worry," she said. "There's no shortage of drugs to keep me flying high. I suppose I should have told them about my hip before they gave me X-57. Oh well, too late now."

It was meant as a joke, but it got Jax thinking: how had the government prioritized who got vaccinated? Only a small proportion of the military personnel based in Colorado Springs had gotten theirs, and yet all of Echo Company did. What about people with medical conditions? Diabetics, for example: if they survived Eko, they'd still face a horrible future once the insulin supply ran out, which wouldn't be long after the power system went dark for good and refrigeration failed.

He gave his head an internal shake. Madness lay down that road. Not unlike the subject they were here to discuss.

Beckett laced her fingers on the table in front of her and looked at them all earnestly. "So," she said. "Dead bodies. Lots of them."

The others exchanged glances, as if looking for permission to laugh, so Jax smiled. They had a lot of grim subjects to talk about, and getting bogged down in misery would be easy to do. As ghoulish as it sounded, they had to maintain a sense of humor about things or they risked losing their sanity.

"Do you have any numbers?" he asked.

"Some." Beckett looked around at the others. "Are you all ready to hear this? It's not good."

They nodded, though Jax wondered if anyone could possibly be ready to hear the details of the end of the world.

"All right, let's get on with it." She riffled through a stack of papers. "The medical experts we've met with—there are a half-dozen civilian doctors and a nurse practitioner in addition to nine doctors and fourteen nurses from the forces—believe the first wave of Eko is over. For all intents and purposes, everyone who was going to die of the virus has died."

Jax breathed his way through a wave of nausea that suddenly rose in his chest. If this middle-aged bureaucrat could get through it, he could.

"The metro population of Colorado Springs prior to Eko was in the neighborhood of 800,000," Beckett continued. "Of those, about 45,000 were military personnel. Our current numbers—these are estimates, obviously; we don't have the manpower for a physical count yet—are around 15,000 civilians and 1,800 military."

Jax felt a chill as he recalled his talk with Archer just a week earlier: these numbers were the same as the ones he'd had to absorb then. He'd never discussed them with anyone else, so they were coming as a shock to the rest of the room. Maggie and Carly had gone white, while Ruben was running a hand down his face. Across the table, Fujita busied himself with scribbling on papers.

"A very small proportion of those infected—far less than one percent—have proved capable of surviving," said Beckett. "The virus kicks the living shit out of them, and they're weak as kittens afterwards—plus they end up with two different-colored eyes out of the deal—but they live. We estimate about fifty or so people fall in that category."

Ruben raised a hand. "I may not be great at math, but I can count. You're saying we've got three-quarters of a million bodies out there in that city?"

"And the surrounding area," Beckett nodded. "Approximately. We know that a small percentage of people left the city, going God knows where, but they would be statistically insignificant."

Jax took another deep breath. Maggie and Carly seemed to be making their way through the revelation, though neither looked ready to speak just yet.

"And it's our job to dispose of them," he said. "I know it sounds like the equivalent of digging to China with a spoon, but it's the reality we're faced with."

"Just playing devil's advocate," said Ruben. "But—"

"Devil's advocate?" Jax smirked. "You?"

Ruben gave him a withering look. "What if we just left them where they are? Just abandon the city and bring the survivors to the bases?"

Beckett shook her head. "Brass wants the city cleared. If we're going to hope for some kind of long-term recovery from this, we need access to the housing, the power plants, the infrastructure."

"And we don't have the luxury of waiting," said Jax. "At the very least, we have to get started on digging immediately; the ground will be frozen in probably ten weeks. And the longer we wait to start, the messier the job will be."

He was glad he didn't have to spell it out for them.

Beckett continued: "We'll be able to clear the bases fairly quickly because the bodies are essentially warehoused. The situation—let's just say things got ugly in the end. Rows of people lying on coats on the floors. The survivors who stayed with those people have a special place in heaven, as far as I'm concerned.

"Again, at the risk of being blunt, we can use bulldozers for those bodies. After that, we'll move on to the hospitals, though they had been regularly disposing of victims via incineration until—well, until things got really bad and there weren't enough people left to do it."

She paused to let everyone process that. Jax could see her throat working, meaning she wasn't as immune to the effects of her job as she liked others to think. For his part, Fujita hadn't looked up from his papers since he sat down.

"Those two stages will likely take us up to when the snow flies, depending on how many recruits we get, which we'll be discussing. Come winter, we can start the secondary job of clearing the neighborhoods. That will require a house-by-house search, which will likely take several months."

Ruben held up a hand again, only this time it was trembling a bit.

"Pardon me, but I just have to say this out loud because it keeps going through my brain: *Fuck. Me.*" He shook his head, eyes wide. "I mean seriously, just fuck me running, man. This is just fucking—I don't know. Do you feel me on this?"

"*I* feel you, Lieutenant," said Fujita, startling the rest of the people in the room. "Every fucking time I look at these papers, all I can see is the word 'fuck' running over and over in my head." He turned to Beckett. "I'm sorry, Captain, it's just the truth."

"This guy gets it," Ruben said. "*He* knows."

"We *all* know, Lieutenant," said Beckett. "It just gets easier after a while. I've personally spent a good hour a day for the last four days just curled up in a ball on my bed, sobbing. I'm not ashamed of it. How else am I supposed to deal with this?"

"Thank God," Carly sighed shakily. "I thought I was the only one."

Maggie held up her hand. "I had a breakdown in my cruiser on the way to this meeting."

They all looked at each other sheepishly for a moment before breaking into hysterical giggles. Tears squirted from every eye as their chests hitched. Jax joined them; it felt good to finally talk about how ridiculous it all was, how alien. How outside the realm of human experience.

The laughter and tears died out after a minute or so, which Jax thought was actually not bad. If Beckett was right, it would get easier as they moved forward.

"Okay," Beckett said with a sigh. "Now that we've had our catharsis break, we can talk about logistics. Namely: how the hell are we going to get the manpower we need to do the job?"

Jax nodded. "That's where we come in. Our team's orders are to connect with the public and act as a conduit for orders from the president and his advisors."

"Well," said Maggie, "you're going to have to liaise your ass off if you want to get the people of Colorado Springs to help you with *anything* right now. I think our little field trip downtown the other day was a pretty telling example of what to expect."

"Not necessarily." Jax had known she would bring that up. "That was, what, twenty people? And as you yourself pointed out, they were drunk and letting off steam. They all left without anyone getting hurt."

She nodded. "They also weren't faced with a literal mountain of dead bodies. Some of whom they'll no doubt recognize."

"So what do you suggest?" Jax shrugged. "I'm open to anything at this point."

Carly raised a tentative hand, and Jax pointed to her.

"I took a marketing course in college," she said. "Have you ever heard of WIFM and KISS?"

Ruben frowned. "Whiff 'em and kiss?"

"It's short for What's In It For Me, and Keep It Simple, Stupid. It's applying psychology principals to marketing campaigns."

"How does that apply here?" asked Jax.

"I see where she's going," Beckett nodded. "We need to come up with a simple reason for them to get involved. Convince them that it's in their best interests."

"Why don't you just order them to do it?" Maggie asked with a hint of what Jax thought was defiance. "From what Capt. Booth has told me, the new republic is run by the army, and people better get on board with that. Not getting shot would be in their best interests."

Jax shook his head. "We will not win this battle at the end of a sword, or down the barrel of a rifle."

"What?"

"Those were President Fletcher's last words from his final broadcast, before Air Force One was shot down. His last request of the American people was to cooperate with each other."

Maggie gave him a crooked grin. "If I recall correctly, he also told us in that speech that America was under martial law. We've seen plenty of evidence of *that*."

"The two don't have to be mutually exclusive," said Jax. "We can ask first and order later, if asking doesn't work."

She nodded, eyebrows raised. "It did work with the crowd at the mall fire," she admitted. "To a degree, anyway."

“All right, then,” he said. “Let’s see if we can’t get a sales pitch put together to recruit some apprentice gravediggers.” He grinned. “And if that doesn’t work, we tell them to start digging their own.”

The line didn’t elicit the laughs he was hoping for. In hindsight, he was glad about that.

22

Rob Taylor had already learned a lot from Nick Roth by the time he joined the crowd gathered outside a pair of army tents in Wasson Park. It was around noon and the soldiers were cooking up hot dogs on a half-dozen Coleman grills. The smell of roasting pseudo-meat was maddening, and Rob thought it, combined with the postcard-perfect weather, was almost enough to make him forget that society had recently collapsed.

Roth's instructions were clear: just observe, don't engage. But after days of eating nothing but cold Pop Tarts and Chef Boy-R-Dee, Rob just couldn't resist the free lunch.

He approached one of the folding tables and picked two dogs on a paper plate. As he doused them with ketchup from a Costco-sized dispenser, he asked the Asian-looking soldier behind the table where the buns had come from.

"Everything I've seen in the stores is totally moldy," he said. He knew he was *engaging*, but he was also curious.

"There's a supply of frozen stores at Cheyenne Mountain," the guy said. "The brass decided this was a special occasion, so they brought 'em out for you folks."

Rob raised a dog in thanks and made his way to where the crowd stood, eating and talking with people in fatigues. He took a seat on an old bus bench on the sidewalk a few yards away so he could listen without being noticed. Up the street, he saw the little coffee shack he used to sometimes go to, where the baristas wore lingerie and sexy costumes when they served you. He supposed they were all dead now. Shame.

"So you can see what I'm talking about," said a sandy-haired dude in a green beret. Rob had grown up in Colorado Springs and knew that meant Special Forces. "The sooner we get the task underway, the sooner we can get folks into their homes."

The crowd—Rob estimated about fifty people—nodded and ate their hot dogs. "How do you decide who gets what?" one person asked through a mouthful of food.

"Lottery system," said the soldier. "First picked get first pick."

"Even those big acreages out on Fontenero?"

"We'll probably have to keep it confined to certain neighborhoods, but possibly."

Rob listened a while longer. The guy was talking about recruiting people for work crews to clear out all the dead bodies that were lying around now. In return, they'd get first pick of the houses in certain parts of the city after things were cleaned up. The army was already looking into how to get the solar power plant at the U.S. Air Force Academy north of the city running at full capacity to feed power to those homes.

That actually sounded pretty good to Rob, despite what Roth had been saying.

"What about those who can't help?" an older woman asked. "My back isn't in any shape for that kind of work. And, to be honest, I think I'd throw up."

"We need people in all sorts of capacities," said the soldier. "Not just physical. We'll find work for anyone who signs up. And there'll be more to come; once we've taken a dent out of the removal, we'll start recruiting a hunting team to stock up on fresh meat for the winter. Come spring, we'll need to get the water treatment plant working again. No one will be bored in Colorado Springs unless they want to be."

That made Rob think of Roth's talk of slavery. What if people didn't *want* to collect corpses? Call it the "removal" if you want, but that's what is was: picking up dead people. What if he just wanted to find himself a house and live in it? There was plenty of food and water for everybody that was left, if the army didn't march in and confiscate it all.

And the *people* didn't cause all this to happen. For all they knew, it was the government's fault.

An odd movement in his peripheral vision caught Rob's attention. It was the weird woman he'd met near his motel—the one who kept talking about oranges—staggering over to where the crowd was standing. As she pushed her way through the people to get to the soldier, Rob noted that she hadn't changed her clothes since the first time he'd seen her. She looked awful.

"Ma'am," the soldier said. "Are you all right?"

The woman started asking him if they had oranges in the tent. Christ, she was a broken record. And she looked like shit. The guy put an arm around her shoulder and called out to someone named Carly. A moment later, a strawberry blonde in fatigues emerged from the second tent.

"I'm sorry, folks, we have to take care of this lady," the soldier said.

"Do I have to sign up today?" a man asked.

"All you have to do is enjoy your hot dogs and think about it. We're going to be hitting different neighborhoods every day at noon for the next week. There's a schedule of locations on the table there. Come meet us any time, and get another hot dog for your trouble."

He and the blonde took Orange Lady into the tent, leaving the people to talk amongst themselves: *should get extra lottery entries if you sign up first... I don't know if my Lori's body is still at Fort Carson, if I saw it there I might lose my mind... least it's something to do, I'm bored outta my skull... beer at my place, if you want to stop by... might as well sign up while I'm here...*

Rob picked up one of the schedules from the table. The Asian guy smiled at him, but Rob ignored him. He suddenly remembered somebody saying that this whole thing was China's fault.

Noon every day. Roth would be interested in this intel for sure. Rob was happy to have actually accomplished something on his reconnaissance mission. He felt like a spy, and as he wandered away from the park toward his new hangout, he wondered what else he'd be called upon to do.

~

"GOOD THING there was some Xanax in that first-aid kit," Carly said as she joined Jax outside the tent. Inside, the woman had collapsed on the ground, so they propped her head up on a stack of coats.

"What's her story?" Jax asked. "Is she sick?"

"I don't think so. She hasn't eaten, obviously, but I think she's had some kind of dissociative break."

"English, Carly," said Jax. "We didn't all take college psychology."

"I'm far from an expert on it," she said. "But it's generally described as pulling away from reality to deal with an overwhelmingly stressful situation. The person doesn't allow themselves to connect with something that they can't deal with."

"I guess that makes sense. Did you get anything out of her?"

"Her name is Anna, and she's looking for orange slices to take to her son's soccer practice."

Jax winced. "Jesus. And yet, when I think about it, I'm surprised we haven't seen more of it."

Rachel's beautiful face filled his mind's eye, unbidden, and he felt a stab in his guts. He wondered if maybe a little dissociation might not be a good thing. He noticed tears welling in Carly's eyes, too.

"I still don't know what happened to my parents," she whispered. "I mean, I have to assume they're dead. Right? But what if they aren't?" She pointed to the dispersing crowd. "All of these people survived, and they weren't vaccinated."

Jax shook his head. "I wish I had advice, but I don't."

She brightened at that; he could practically see a light bulb appear above her head. "Maybe we should be doing something about that."

"How so?"

"There has to be someone with psychology training under the mountain." The wheels were spinning behind her eyes. "We should be helping people get through this. At the very least, we could all be crying together instead of separately."

He nodded. It was a good idea. "Maybe see if there's any clergy we can bring out on these little jaunts, from the mountain or a civilian, doesn't matter which."

"I don't know if I'd go that far," Carly said with a frown. "God and I aren't exactly on speaking terms right now, if you get what I mean."

Jax chuckled in spite of himself. "Yeah, I wouldn't want to be His receptionist these days."

The two of them scanned the area. The crowd was mostly gone and Fujita was packing up the condiments. Every last hot dog had been eaten.

"Is it possible we actually did some good here today?" Carly asked.

"I'd like to think so," said Jax. "And who knows? Maybe we can do some more for people like Anna in there. At least we're trying."

As they started taking down the tent, Jax tried hard not to listen to the voice deep down in his mind that kept telling him the road to hell was paved with good intentions.

23

Fujita's hot dog stand was packed, thanks to word getting around about the daily lunch sign-ups. Jax had even seen a few of the schedules they'd handed out over the past three days taped to light standards and stapled to public message boards (one of the boards had been covered with the words IT'S COMING in red spray paint, which sent a chill through Jax's guts) and they seemed to be working. This afternoon had seen almost seventy civilians so far. They might have had even more if the overcast sky hadn't been threatening rain.

Ruben was chatting with a handful of people as they ate. Jax envied his friend—he'd always had the gift of the gab and was able to talk in just about any situation. Jax joined the group just as a twenty-something man with a thick beard and cracked eyeglasses was speaking.

"Where did the virus come from, anyway?" the man asked Ruben. "I heard the Chinese."

"Actually, I think Capt. Booth here is better able to field that question." He grinned, prompting an insincere smile from Jax in return.

"That's an excellent question," he said. "In fact, our intelligence indicates that Eko was actually developed as a bioweapon by the

North Korean regime. For whatever reason, the developers apparently thought they could somehow keep it contained to a small area, but of course, we saw what happened."

A few people nodded knowingly, others shook their heads. A couple of people said "I knew it" at almost exactly the same time.

"So this isn't just here in Colorado?" asked a black woman in a pink sweatsuit and running shoes. Jax had noticed that comfort seemed to be the new fashion among the civilian survivors. He couldn't blame them—he wouldn't have been wearing fatigues himself if it wasn't expected of him.

"No, ma'am. Our intel indicates this is a worldwide phenomenon. We saw the beginnings of it in Germany ourselves before we returned to the States."

The woman looked crestfallen. "I kept hoping that we could just go someplace else. Someplace where this didn't happen."

"I'm sorry, ma'am," said Carly, joining them. "We know it's been hard on everyone. That's why we're offering counselling to anyone who asks for it. We want everyone here in Colorado Springs to weather the storm and come out the other side. So let us know if you need anything, or even if you just want to talk."

There were murmurs in the group before a bald man with an oddly babyish face spoke up: "I heard the president is here in the city. Is that true?"

Jax was prepared for the question. Raines had told him not to lie to the public about what was happening, unless he had no other choice.

"President Raines is here, yes," he said. "In fact, Colorado Springs is the current seat of government for the United States."

Baby Face let out a low whistle. "So it's true—Fletcher *is* dead?"

Jax nodded. "Air Force One was shot down over Nevada by someone working on behalf of the Chinese government. That person also assassinated Gen. Marcus Chase, the Secretary of Defense, before being killed himself."

He felt Ruben's hand on his shoulder. "It was Captain Booth here who took out the assassin," his friend said proudly.

Eyes widened among the crowd while Jax tried his damndest to not look as uncomfortable as he felt.

"Seriously?" Baby Face asked. "That's crazy! Like a movie or something. And *you* killed the guy? Seriously?"

"Seriously," Jax said. It was almost true—only the characters had been playing each other's parts.

Keep telling yourself that, Jackson.

"Marcus Chase was a goddamn hero to this country," said a middle-aged man who looked like he'd been wearing the same clothes for several days. "Fucking Chinese. First they steal all our jobs, then they do this. It's crazy."

The woman in the sweatsuit moved closer to Jax. "Well, I for one am glad we have people like you here to look out for us," she said, reaching out to take his hand. The adulation made him supremely uncomfortable. "You people are the real heroes."

There was a murmur of general agreement in the crowd. Each time he heard that sound over the last few days, Jax felt a little bit more like they were accomplishing something. That there was some hope for this this fragile new republic they were tasked with building.

Hell, the fact that there'd been no more reports of armed civilians stalking the streets was enough of a step in the right direction just on its own.

"Careful, folks," Maggie said with a sardonic grin. "Let's not give these fellas swelled heads or they won't be able to fit into their helmets."

"The real heroes have been this city's own first responders," said Jax. "People like Sheriff Stubbs here, every other person who did everything they could to keep order during chaos. We owe each and every one of those who didn't make it a debt we can never repay."

A smattering of applause from the crowd seemed to take Maggie off guard, which gave Jax some degree of satisfaction. *Jesus, I really* am *turning into a politician.*

When she glanced over at him, there was a look in her eyes he'd never seen there before. Gratitude, maybe? Or was it something else?

"Hey, Captain," Ruben called from one of the tents. "I need your help here. Lt. Grant, you too, please."

Jax saw Ruben standing next to a man in his twenties with a mop of brown hair and a faraway stare. He thought the guy looked familiar, but couldn't quite place him. He excused himself and made his way to Ruben and Carly at the tent.

"What's up?" he asked.

"Our man here tells me he's having some troubles," said Ruben. "Wondered if we could maybe help him out."

"I'm sure we can," Carly chirped. "That's what we're here for."

"That's good," said Ruben, grinning wide. "Because this gentleman is worried that the Chinese government is beaming signals into his brain."

The young fellow continued to stare into the distance, barely acknowledging his two new companions. Jax and Carly exchanged glances without altering their expressions, which Jax considered a minor miracle. Inside his mind, he sighed deeply.

"All right, sir," he said. "How about we go inside this tent here and talk about things?"

The guy nodded. Jax turned to Carly and whispered: "We're going to be late with this. Better tell Fujita to radio in to the mountain and find someone to pick up Hayley from school. Then get back here double-time; I'm not ready to tackle something like this on my own, and we both know Lambert isn't going to be any help."

She clamped down on a smile and headed towards Fujita's table as Jax put a hand on their new patient's shoulder and led him inside the tent.

"By the way, sir," he asked, "what should we call you?"

"Joe," the guy mumbled.

That was a lie. His real name was Rob Taylor, and he was on a secret mission.

SURE GLAD *I spent those four years at the Citadel before I signed up,* Carey

Fujita moped as he collected stray paper plates left behind by the throng of people who'd finally dispersed. Like the old recruitment commercials used to say: Be All That You Can Be. For him, that now meant serve all the hot dogs you can serve. Order all the after-school rides for your commander's kid that you can order.

"Need a hand, sir?"

Fujita looked up from his crouch to see a kid in airman's fatigues standing over him with an easy smile.

"Can always use an extra hand if you're okay with clean-up duty," Fujita said. "Though I can't say I know why we bother."

The kid grabbed a black garbage bag from the table and followed Fujita around, picking up whatever he didn't. Fujita figured he must be almost a raw recruit—couldn't have been older than nineteen.

"Begging your pardon, sir," the kid said, scratching his scalp. Fujita noted it had the red bumps of a fresh shave. "But I figure we might as well start over with a cleaner slate than we got left to us, you know?"

Fujita straightened up and and yanked the ties on the bag tight. "I have to admit I hadn't thought of it that way. I like your attitude. What's your name, Airman?"

"Payne, sir," the kid lied with a grin.

"Who do you report to?"

"Lt. Grant, sir."

"Huh," said Fujita. "She actually just left. Asked me to radio the mountain to send someone over to the resort to pick up our company commander's kid from the school at 1500 hours. Take her back to the mountain." He tilted his head. "You wouldn't be...?"

The kid, whose real name was Malcolm Austin, shrugged.

"I'd be happy to do it, sir," he said. "Just let the school know I'm coming and I'll go grab her."

~

BY THE END of the school day, Hayley was almost completely sure that she had made a new friend.

Becca Holt was a couple of years older than her, and she acted kind of weird sometimes, but they had bonded over magnetic clay sculptures that they had spent the last couple of hours building. It started out as boring—they weren't allowed to play with anything that used electricity because they were supposed to save energy—but by the time school was over, Hayley found herself actually wanting to take her sculpture back to her bunk to finish it.

She and Becca had discovered they had a lot in common, thanks to Ms. Sidley. The teacher had sat down with the two of them and talked for a while, then asked them some questions. Becca told them her mom was a nurse, just like Hayley's mom. She was working at a hospital in Colorado Springs. Her dad was a soldier, like Jax, except he worked at Fort Carson. Becca's mom had died, too, but not from the virus. She had died cleaning her dad's gun. Now she and her dad lived at the hotel where the school was. Becca said her dad didn't talk a lot any more.

Then there was Brady Puckett. His parents had died from the virus, and he had gotten sick, too. Then he got better, but now his eyes were two different colors, which was weird—Hayley never knew which one to look at when she was talking to him. Ms. Sidley was his guardian now, just like Jax was hers. Ms. Sidley said there would be a lot more kids coming to the school in the next few days from the city.

"Hayley!" Ms. Sidley called from the door of the big room they used for the school.

"I have to go now," Hayley said, looking wistfully at the Tyrannosaurus she was building with the clay. She couldn't put it into words, but for some reason creating things made her feel better these days.

Becca stood and hugged her fiercely. "See you tomorrow."

"Yup. I hope your dad is doing okay today."

"Me, too," she sighed. "He never is, but I always hope he will be."

Hayley waved to a few other kids before she got to the door and Ms. Sidley. She liked her teacher a lot, probably more than anyone else besides Jax, Ruben and Val. When she got to the door, though,

Jax was nowhere to be seen. Instead there was a teenager in fatigues who looked like he'd just shaved his head.

"Jax can't pick you up today, Hayley," Ms. Sidley said with a smile. "This is Airman Payne. He'll take you back to the mountain and Jax will meet you when he's off duty. Okay?"

Hayley nodded. The airman smiled at her and reached out a hand. "Nice to meet you, Miss Moore."

She took his hand and gave it a brisk shake. Aside from mild disappointment at not seeing Jax, she didn't give the situation a second thought. She'd been surrounded by soldiers for over two weeks now; what was one more?

Airman Payne led her out of the hotel to a white car that didn't look like any of the vehicles she had seen military people drive. It was low to the ground and wide, and there were only two seats in it.

"Have you ever seen a car like this, Hayley?" he asked. He pressed a button on the fob and the doors opened upwards, like wings.

She shook her head, wide-eyed. "What is it?"

"It's called a Chrysler Nighthawk. It can go up to 300 miles per hour."

"Is it a gas car?" she asked. "I've heard of them. They're supposed to be faster than regular cars."

He grinned. "You're pretty smart. Only rich people could afford them because gas is so expensive. But now it doesn't really matter anymore, does it? I just took this one. No one's using it."

Hayley wondered about that. Her mom had always taught her that stealing was wrong. But things were different now, weren't they? And it wasn't her place to question grown-ups, even if they were practically kids themselves, like Airman Payne.

She sank into the passenger seat, feeling the special foam mold itself around her. The door dropped down automatically as the seatbelt crawled over her shoulder and clicked into place on its own.

"Pretty cool, huh?" Airman Payne asked as he took his seat.

"Yeah." She was starting to like this car now that she was inside. She imagined herself inside the cockpit of a spaceship of some sort.

Airman Payne hit the ignition and a low rumble growled from the engine. Hayley was used to the whine and hum of electric or hybrid vehicles. This was a new experience for her, to actually hear and *feel* the engine.

"Cool," she breathed.

Airman Payne looked over at her and grinned.

"Wait till we get moving," he said. "You're in for a real adventure this afternoon, Hayley."

24

"It's, like, what if everyone here is a Chinese agent except for me?"

Jax pinched the bridge of his nose. He could tell Ruben was doing his best not to punch the guy, while Carly simply looked baffled. They'd been going through this for more than an hour now.

"That's a pretty big stretch, Joe," he sighed. "Wouldn't you say? I mean, if everyone else was the enemy, what would be the point of trying to make you believe that they weren't? Why wouldn't they just kill you?"

Joe nodded knowingly and jabbed an index finger at them. "Exactly."

Jax shook his head and glanced at his watch: it was after 1630 hours already. Long past when they had planned to be out of here. And they still had to meet up with Fujita back at the resort to go over any registrations from the afternoon.

Carly leaned forward, elbows on her knees. "Look, Joe, are you staying somewhere nearby? Maybe we can check in on you once in a while, make sure everything is okay."

"I'm staying at a mo—uh, I mean, no, I don't have any one place. I, uh, move around a lot."

Ruben tried his hand. "How about tomorrow? We're going to be at the Chapel Hills Mall. Can you meet us there?"

"Maybe," Joe muttered. "I don't know. What time is it?"

"Four-forty," said Jax. "Why? Got an appointment?"

He cursed himself for being snide as soon as the words were out of his mouth, but Jesus, come on. This was getting ridiculous.

Joe stood up and glanced out the door of the tent. Jax followed his gaze and saw the sun starting to make its way to a lower angle on the western horizon.

"I don't," Joe said. "But *you* do."

Ruben rose from his seat and headed warily for the door. Jax's instincts were a few seconds behind his friend's, but he was starting to feel it too.

"What are you talking about?" Ruben asked.

"Guys, now!"

Jax leapt from his own seat and spun to face the door. As he did, he saw Ruben throw Carly behind him and follow suit.

A moment later, their instincts were borne out as a dozen men wearing fatigues and carrying automatic rifles stormed into the tent. Jax's pulse quickened as he recognized HK416s, a couple of Smith & Wesson Creedmors, and some others that shared space on the upper shelves of the gun shops. All of them were pointed at him and his companions. All of them carried the potential for a massacre.

None were pointed at Joe.

Jax took a breath, steeling himself, as he raised his hands. The others did the same; he could see by Carly's face that she was fighting back panic.

A quick scan of the group showed all of their assailants were wearing the blue star and double chevron rank insignia of airmen second class.

"What the fuck is going on here?!" Jax barked. "Stand down now or I'll have you court-martialed!"

The men didn't move or speak, simply stood their ground in formation, weapons trained on the trio.

"I don't recognize any of these men," said Carly. "I could see not recognizing *all* of them, but it's impossible that I don't know *any* of them."

"I think you'll know one, Lieutenant," said a voice from a silhouette in the doorway. The sun was behind him, obscuring his features.

"Wait a minute," Ruben said as the newcomer walked in and away from the bright light. "This isn't right..."

Now that he was in the tent, Jax could make out the muscular frame, the salt-and-pepper hair. He'd never met the man whose place Carly Grant had taken on his team, but he knew who he was looking at.

"Jesus Christ," Carly breathed. Her glowing cheeks stood out in stark contrast with her normally pale skin. *"Col. Roth?"*

The man smiled sheepishly. "Might as well dispense with the formalities now, Carly. We all know I'm not a colonel anymore. I'm just Nick Roth, private citizen." He turned to Jax. "Captain Booth. I've heard good things about you. Sorry I stood you up. Hank Archer must have been pissed about that one."

"Not as pissed as I am right now," Jax growled. "I'll have your ass for this, whatever the hell this is. If these men don't want a repeat of Palmer High, I suggest they drop their weapons right now."

He was still trying to take it all in: no one had reported seeing Roth since the meeting where Archer had put Jax in charge over a week ago. In fact, no one had seemed overly concerned that they couldn't find him, at least as far as Jax knew.

Roth chuckled. "We both know there aren't members of Echo Company lying in wait for us here. This was a perfect ambush." He put an arm around Joe's shoulder. "Thanks to our man Rob here."

Ruben's eyes closed as his head dropped back on his shoulders. "Fuck me," he groaned. "He kept us sitting here until you could get into position."

"But why?" Carly was practically sputtering. "Colonel, what possible reason could you have for doing this? And where did these men get their uniforms?"

"Use your head, Carly," said Roth. "This is Colorado Springs.

There are at least a dozen military supply stores that were just sitting there, waiting to be pillaged."

"That doesn't explain what's going on! Where did you disappear to? They think you deserted!"

Roth stared at her as if she was speaking a foreign language.

"*Of course* I deserted," he said finally. "There was no place for me in the new command structure."

Jax scowled, finally lowering his hands. "How did *you* know? You took off before anyone had a chance to talk to you."

"It's the army or nothing, Captain," said Roth. "We both know that. Look at Major Price: senior ranking marine in the state of Colorado and he's working some shit detail under you."

"What we do is important!" Jax protested.

"Is that right? Like helping 'Joe' here deal with his night terrors?"

Carly's eyes blazed. "Very funny, *Nick*. We're also recruiting civilians to help dig the mass graves we need to bury the hundreds of thousands of dead bodies in and around this city. What have *you* been doing besides getting this band of brothers together?"

"Enough," Jax said. "I don't give a shit if you're working on a revival of The Wizard of Oz. I'm giving you one last chance to get the hell out of here and take your clown crew with you. Archer is in command under the president now, and a guy named Smith has his old job. Believe me, you don't want *that* bastard to catch up with you anywhere."

ROTH SURPRISED JAX BY SMILING. "I know, I heard about the incident in Atlanta. Tell me, Captain, doesn't it seem just the slightest bit odd to you that he ended up where he is?"

It had, of course, but Jax didn't want to give Roth any more fodder for paranoia right now.

"Smith is willing to do what has to be done," he said. "This is a new reality, Roth. A new republic. And if we don't maintain some semblance of order here in Colorado Springs, then there's no hope for the rest of America."

"Says the man who ordered the death of a dozen men at William J. Palmer High School," Roth said. "I'd say Smith has himself a protégé."

Jax felt hot blood rise in his face. Roth's men had remained silent up to that point, but a few were now shaking their heads.

"You think there's an America left to save?" asked a guy who Jax recognized from one of the recruitment rallies. "This shit happened everywhere in the fucking world, you said so yourself. There's no America anymore. There's no *anything* anymore!"

Ruben's clear baritone rang out in the tent. "America isn't a place, you idiot!" he yelled. "It's a *concept!* And If we don't keep it alive, we're all well and truly fucked!"

Jax thought he'd never agreed with his friend more in his life than he did right at that moment.

"Well, then," said Roth, crossing his arms over his chest. "We're all fucked, Lieutenant, because America is over. It died last week, and the world died with it. All that's left is us."

Carly shook her head. "This isn't the Nick Roth I knew," she said. "You didn't join the air force and work your way up to command because you *didn't* believe in America.

"Enough!" Jax barked. "Either shoot now or tell us what this is about. If you don't, I'm walking out of here, and anyone who gets in my way better be ready to die. Is that clear?"

"Does that sound like the *American* thing to say, Lieutenant?" Roth asked Ruben. The smugness in his expression made Jax want to knock his teeth down his throat.

"All right, all right," Roth continued, raising his hands in a gesture of mock surrender. "You win. Obviously there's a reason for this. We need you to drive us to Schriever."

Jax stared at him, angry and dumbfounded. This was all about hitching a ride to a fucking air force base?

"It's a thirty-minute trip and all you'll find at the end is thousands of bodies," he said. "Why the hell would you want to go there? And why do you need us to drive you?"

Roth grinned. "There's a bit more there than just bodies, and technically, I only need *you* to drive me. These two are extraneous."

Carly's face flushed as the realization of what he'd said set in. Ruben scowled beside her and squared himself into a ready position. Nothing was happening to her while he was around.

"That's not what I meant," Roth said when he saw their reactions. "I just meant that you're the only one who's indispensable on this mission, Captain."

"Why? None of you can drive a personnel truck?"

Roth chuckled. "I like your style, Captain. I think under different circumstances we could have been friends."

"You think wrong."

He shrugged. "*C'est la vie*. Anyway, I need you to get us into a specific place at Schriever. Once that happens, you three can go do whatever you want for the rest of your lives and I won't give a single shit."

"What specific place?"

Roth perked up. "I'm glad you asked! It's actually a storage facility near the east end of the parking lot."

Jax blinked. "*What?*"

"That's it. Get us past the guard detail there and you're home free."

"Why is there a guard detail? There's nothing worth stealing at Schriever. You say America is over? Well, I say the air force is over, for the time being, at least."

"I know that," Roth said drily. "There's no aircraft in the building. It's something much more useful."

Jax sighed. "Get to the point."

"It's a cache of weapons that Geoffrey Benton had moved there before he died and Echo Company and the rest arrived in Colorado Springs."

"Bullshit." Jax frowned. "You're out of your mind. There's nothing at Schriever besides aircraft you can't fly and thousands of Eko victims. Everything else has been scavenged for use at Cheyenne Mountain or here in the city."

Roth shrugged. "Then I guess none of this matters. You take us there, we find an empty storage facility and the joke's on us. Then if you follow your current standard operating procedure, you kill all of us and go back home for supper."

"You fucking—"

"Easy, Captain. The sooner we get this over with, the sooner we can all get on with our lives."

Jax shook his head, grinning coldly. "See, that's where you're wrong. You think we're going to go along with this. What are you going to do if we don't? Kill us? You do and Echo Company will be on you like a pack of wolves on a nest of mice. You wouldn't last a day."

He watched as Roth's expression changed. The man took a deep breath, let it out. Where before he'd been almost joking around, now he looked deadly serious.

"All right, Captain," he said. "I was hoping it wouldn't come to this, but you've forced my hand."

Jax scoffed. "Is that right? You've got some leverage on us, do you?"

Roth reached down to his belt, removed a walkie-talkie and turned the dial to activate it. The hiss of static filled the tent until he pressed down on the button on the side.

"Liberty Two, this is Liberty One, over."

Liberty, Jax thought. *Give me a fucking break.*

"Go for Liberty Two, over," said a voice on the other end. Jax felt a flutter in his solar plexus as he recognized it: the kid from the mall riot with the jerry can.

"Do you have the package, over?"

"Affirmative, over."

Roth looked Jax in the eye. "Remember, Captain, this is on you." He handed the radio to him.

"This is Captain Jackson Booth," he barked into the mouthpiece. "And I am seriously pissed off right now, so I suggest you do not fuck with me. What's going on?"

The line hissed static for several long moments until a small voice came across the speaker, quiet as a whisper but powerful enough to freeze his guts solid.

"Jax?" Hayley sobbed. "Are you there? He says he's going to hurt me."

All his rage drained out of him, replaced by cold terror.

25

The van had been easy enough to acquire. It was a twelve-seater Foton, black, sitting on the lot of a dealership near Palmer Park. One of Roth's men shot out the glass of the front door and went through the fobs until he found all the ones with the Mercedes logo, then activated them all until they found the one to the van.

In the rearview camera, Jax saw an SUV appropriated in the same way from the same lot. A pair of armed goons rode in its backseat behind Ruben and Carly as they followed them along Highway 94 east towards Schriever AFB and whatever awaited them there.

It was hardly a scenic drive; the mountains and the lowering sun were all behind them in the west. All that broke up the endless sea of dun and green scrub along the road was the occasional herd of cattle wandering along the barbed wire fences that lined the highway.

"Somebody needs to get out here and start taking care of the cows," Roth said from the passenger seat next to Jax. If not for the SIG Sauer leveled at his ribs, the man could have been just a hitch-hiker who was chatting to pass the time on a particularly boring trip.

"What do you know about it?" Jax muttered.

"Just that it would be stupid not to take advantage of such an easy food supply. If you don't, Colorado is going to have a mighty obese wolf and coyote population."

Jax shook his head. "Disease will kill a lot more of them than predators."

"You sound like you know what you're talking about."

"I grew up on a ranch. East Texas."

Roth grinned. "Who better to take over the operation, then? The Chico Basin Ranch south of Schriever has thousands of head of cattle. Horses, too. They all need looking after, or culling, at least. Seems to me your talents are being wasted, Captain."

"My talent is killing terrorists."

He turned serious. "Is that how you see me?"

"You're holding an innocent child hostage," Jax snarled. "So that I'll help you get your hands on heavy duty military weapons. What do *you* call yourself, Roth? A philanthropist?"

The miles ticked by as Highway 94 unfolded in front of them. Soon they would turn south on Enoch Road, which would take them the last handful of miles to the base.

"You're not seeing the big picture," said Roth. "You're either ignoring it or you're blind, but either way, the result is the same."

"Yeah? What's the big picture?"

"The government is going to pretend that it can still control things. The only way it can do that is to maintain order. The only way to maintain order is by enforcing rules."

"How is that a bad thing?"

Roth shook his head. "Did you not see President Fletcher's final message?"

Jax frowned as he remembered using Fletcher's words only days ago to justify his own actions. But Roth's ideas were skewed—they *did* need to maintain order. Without it, America would simply revert back to the Wild West, where whoever had the most guns made the rules. They couldn't allow that to happen.

"It's a different reality now," he said. "Fletcher didn't know the extent of the virus—"

"Don't kid yourself," said Roth. "America's intelligence community saw Eko coming, believe me. How do you think they managed to get a vaccine?"

"Yeah, they got a vaccine, way too late for it to stop the end of the world."

"Ah, but they managed to get it to the military people first, didn't they?"

Jax glared at him. "Who else would you give it to? They needed soldiers to maintain order after the collapse. It's the only possible hope for survival."

"Whose survival?" Roth shrugged. "Civilians? There's more than enough preserved food and bottled water sitting around for the survivors of Eko. There are, what, 15,000 people left in Colorado Springs? There was enough food in the city to feed 800,000 before the collapse. Simple math says they'll survive. Sure, it won't be the most luxurious life, but they'll have food, shelter, all the basics they need."

"What are you trying to say?"

Roth shrugged. "I'm wondering how that situation is going to be made better by having a government and an army in place."

"Says the man who's about to steal a cache of weapons from that military. How do they fit into this new return to the natural state?"

"Good point," said Roth. "Cicero probably wouldn't have approved. But Cicero lived in ancient Rome, not post-collapse America. If we're going to go our own way, we need to be able to keep the Archers and Smiths at bay. We'd have to be idiots not to arm ourselves."

Jax slowed the van as he saw the sign for Enoch Road. He hit his right turn signal before he even realized what he was doing. Old habits died hard.

"Had to let Carly and Lt. Lambert know we were turning?" Roth taunted.

Jax ignored it. "If we're going to have any hope of rebuilding the republic, we need structure in place, not anarchy."

"Says who? How do you know that America wouldn't be better off as a series of independent states all across this great land, from sea to shining sea? People returning to their roots, leaving technology and government behind and just living simply, in peace?"

"We had that for thousands of years," said Jax. "Ever read a history book? There's a war on pretty much every page."

Roth raised a finger like a professor who's just been challenged by a student. "Yes, indeed! But those were in places where there were a whole lot of people crammed into a small space. America has nothing *but* space now, and no shortage of resources. When everyone has enough, there's no reason for them to fight."

"The Communists in the Soviet Union preached about everyone having enough. That was cold comfort to the millions of people Stalin killed."

"That's a completely different situation," Roth said.

"What about American Indians? They killed each other all the time, even before the white man showed up, and they had nothing *but* space."

Roth sighed. "Okay, Captain, I get it. We're not on the same page. We'll agree to disagree."

Jax grinned. "No, I'll agree to put a bullet in your head the second I get the chance, Roth. You can agree to whatever the hell you want."

"All I want is to live my life free from tyranny," he said, but there was no irony there, no sneer in his voice this time. "Maybe you want someone ordering you to rebuild the world according to their ideals, Captain; that's up to you. I don't. I may not be from New Hampshire, but the motto 'live free or die' still means something to me. And bowing to the unelected masters of this new republic of yours is *not* what I consider freedom."

Sunset was just beginning as the first view of Schriever appeared on the horizon. Jax checked his rear camera to make sure Ruben and Carly were keeping up. Behind him in the van, the ten members of Roth's ad hoc militia stared out the windows; some fidgeted with their rifles, a few rocked back and forth in their seats. One dug a finger into his left nostril almost to the first knuckle.

As they passed the visitor's center and followed Falcon Parkway toward the main base, Roth leaned closer to Jax.

"You can see the building as soon as we enter the parking lot," he said. "There will be two guards, both with M16s."

"And then what? You kill them? But you're not terrorists—you said so yourself."

"Who said anything about killing them? That's why we needed you for this—to convince them to open it up."

"Why do you need to do that?"

"Because the building is locked tight, and just in case anyone gets past the guards, there's a failsafe explosive charge set up around the perimeter of the building."

Jax chewed on that. Why was there a weapons cache in the first place? And in the aftermath of the collapse, why was there so much effort to keep it away from people?

Roth smiled. "I can see the wheels moving behind your eyes, Captain. Good. But for now, we need to focus on the task at hand."

"What makes you think they'll do anything for *me*?" asked Jax.

"Don't be so modest. You're the man who killed the mole who shot down Air Force One and assassinated Marcus Chase. You're a hero, Captain."

A jolt of unease ran through Jax's belly and he wondered if there was any way Roth could possibly know the truth. Before he could give it any more thought, they entered the parking lot. In the distance, he saw what Roth had been talking about: a metal shoebox, maybe 20,000 square feet. A pair of ten-foot hangar doors covered a good chunk of the front of the building.

Sure enough, two armed men in fatigues stood guard next to a fleet of trucks parked nearby. The yellow eagles on their shoulders identified them as privates. As the van approached, the men moved forward and raised their hands for him to stop. He checked behind him: as per the plan, Ruben and Carly had stayed back at the entrance to the parking lot.

The guard closest to the driver's side approached him slowly, almost as if he were bored by the duty. Jax rolled down his window and flashed what he hoped was a winning smile.

"Evening, Private," he said. "How'd you snag this primo detail?"

"Identify please, sir."

"Capt. Jackson Booth, here on orders from Col. Smith. We need to get inside."

The guard, a swarthy fellow who appeared to be in his late twenties, looked like he'd just been slapped.

"*The* Capt.Booth?" he asked, eyes wide. "The guy who killed the mole in Cheyenne Mountain?"

Jax smiled but it felt more like a grimace. "The same."

The private turned to his colleague, who was standing on the passenger side of the van. "Hey, man!" he called. "This is Capt. *Booth*, man!"

Now it was the other guy's turn to let his eyes pop.

"No shit!" he said, then cleared his throat and saluted. "Jeremiah Perry, sir. It's an honor."

The other seemed to shake himself out of a daze and followed suit. "Begging your pardon, sir. Joe Stratch. I'm very glad to meet you, sir."

"Privates." Jax nodded and returned their salutes. "I've heard nothing but good things about you two."

The men glanced at each other and visibly swelled with pride.

"What can we do for you, sir?" asked Perry.

"We're here to do an emergency inventory. Just need to get in. There's sixteen of us, so shouldn't take more than an hour. When do you men get relieved?"

"Not till 2300 hours," said Stratch.

"We'll be gone long before then." Jax reached into the pocket of his seat and pulled out a brown paper bag. "Hey, either of you hungry? We've got some leftover hotdogs. They're not exactly hot anymore, but..."

"Yessir!" Perry all but yelped. "Thank you, sir. I'd kill for a hot dog."

"Me, too, sir," said Stratch. "I'm getting awful tired of bean soup and spaghetti."

The men shouldered their rifles and Jax handed Stratch the bag as he exited the van. On the passenger side, Roth got out and opened the side door to let the men out of the back. Six of them took a loose formation around him while the others hung back. They all left their weapons in the van.

Perry gobbled his hot dog greedily. "Jesus, that's good," he said, showing off a mouthful of half-chewed food. "Who'd have thought you could miss tube steak so much?"

"That's what *she* said," Stratch joked, then snorted a laugh and almost choked on his own meal.

Jax chuckled along and clapped Stratch on the back as they headed to the hangar doors. "Settle down, there, Private. Smith would have my ass if I went back and told him one of his men had choked on a tube steak."

That prompted a snort from Perry beside them.

"Christ, Perry!" Jax said, still laughing. "What'd I just say? We need every able-bodied man we have right now!"

"Yessir. Thanks again for the chow, sir."

As they reached the doors, Stratch and Perry went to either side and simultaneously punched in a code. They glanced at each other, nodded, then each pressed another button in tandem. A second later, the heavy steel doors rolled sideways. Inside, Jax could see floor-to-ceiling shelves lined with racks of semi-auto rifles, pistols and crates of ammunition. There had to have been a thousand or more weapons and millions of rounds of ammo.

In another area were a dozen grenade launchers and corresponding crates of grenades. Ten pairs of crates next to those read HEAT, which stood for High Explosive Anti-Tank. It meant the boxes housed shaped-charge warheads that could be used on their own or with a variety of launching weapons. Given the lack of that type of weapon here, Jax assumed it would be for the latter.

"Do you need any help, sir?" asked Perry. "It's actually pretty boring duty. No one ever comes out here."

Jax glanced at Roth as he entered, expecting to see his eyes dancing like a kid on Christmas morning. Instead, the man looked grim. Jax thought he might see that expression on the face of a surgeon heading into a complex operation that had little chance of succeeding. Again, for just a moment, he wondered what had driven the man to this point.

"Thank you, gentlemen," said Roth. "But you've already done more than enough."

With a raised hand, he drew out the six men who had stayed at the van. They emerged from the other side with their weapons drawn and advanced on the stunned soldiers.

"Sir?" Stratch asked nervously. "What's going on?"

"Just do what they tell you and you'll be all right," Jax said through clenched teeth.

"This is what's known as a heist," Roth said evenly. "We want the weapons, not you."

Another gesture and two men removed the soldiers' weapons. Stratch and Perry stood against a wall, hands in the air, as two of Roth's men kept their own rifles trained on them.

The SUV carrying Ruben, Carly and their two passengers pulled up silently alongside them. They got out and joined the group inside the warehouse.

"Now what?" asked Ruben.

"Now we wait," said Roth.

"For what?"

"For the next part of the plan."

26

In the distance they heard the growling of a powerful gasoline engine. It grew louder over a handful of seconds, until they saw a vehicle screaming through the lane of the parking lot towards them. For a few alarming seconds, Jax thought the car would keep on going and drive straight into the building at full speed.

About a hundred yards out, the car—a low, wide sports model—suddenly turned to the left and drifted towards them, brakes screeching, leaving a trail of burnt rubber on the asphalt between the rows of dead vehicles as it spun a full 360 degrees before coming to a stop.

"For Christ's sake," Roth growled. He jogged toward the car as its gull-wing doors clicked open.

The man whose voice Jax had recognized on the radio stepped out of the driver's seat. He'd shaved his head, but Jax could still make out that it was the same kid who'd tried to stare them down at the strip mall. Bile rose in his throat at the thought of this bastard next to his Hayley.

The girl stepped shakily out of the passenger side and Jax instinctively broke ranks and sprinted towards her.

"Stop him!" Roth called, and two of his men drew their rifles on Jax.

"We'll shoot!" one of them hollered. "Don't think we won't!"

Jax slowed and raised his hands. He believed them, even if they hadn't shown any propensity for violence so far. He had to believe them if he wanted to ensure everyone made it out of this alive.

"Jax!" Hayley wailed. "Are you okay?"

"I'm fine, kiddo," he said, trying to look and sound calm. The coolness that usually overtook him in combat hadn't come yet; in fact, his guts were popping like a live wire. "What about you?"

The red rims of her eyes told him she'd been crying. Jax glared at the driver, willing him to die.

"The drive was scary," she said. "But I'm all right."

"God *damn* it, Malcolm." Roth was quietly dressing down the kid. "We need to keep a low profile."

"Whatever, man," said Malcolm, who clearly wasn't amused with the conversation. "These are *my* people, not yours. Remember that." He stormed into the warehouse.

Roth nodded in Jax's direction. "You can go to her if you want."

He jogged in Hayley's direction, but she sprinted toward him and crossed the space between them in two seconds flat. Jax instinctively dropped to one knee as she leapt into his arms. As he closed them around her, he thought he'd never understood the meaning of the word relief until that moment.

"I was brave," she sobbed in his ear. "Just like you."

"I know you were, honey." He clamped down on a wave of his own emotions. There was no place for them, not right now. "I'm proud of you."

He stood and took her by the hand, leading her over to Ruben and Carly. They both hugged her in turn. Three of Roth's men approached, weapons drawn, and ordered them into the building.

"What's happening?" Hayley asked, clutching Jax's hand again.

"I'd like to know the answer to that myself," Ruben said quietly. "They're going to load this up and just drive away? Sounds too simple. Why are we even here?"

Jax brought them up to speed about using him to get the guards to open up. The fact the men were still alive almost made him believe that Roth was closer to Robin Hood than terrorist, at least in the man's own mind.

An air force transport truck that had been sitting in the parking lot suddenly fired to life as someone inside let out a satisfied whoop. Jax saw Roth grin as the truck started driving toward them.

"Awesome," Malcolm said with a snide grin. "We got a truck. Now what, plan man?"

The obvious discord between Roth and the kid could come in handy, Jax thought. He'd just have to wait for an opening.

"We need to get these on the truck," said Roth, pointing at the weapons. "That forklift over there is probably running low on juice. If the government had sprung for new ones, we could be out of here in no time. Unfortunately, they just retrofitted the old diesel ones to electric with cheap Chinese batteries that don't hold their charge. So we load as much of the heavy stuff as we can before it runs out, then switch to manual."

Malcolm's eyes narrowed. "What do you mean, manual?"

"We load it by hand," Roth said. "Jesus, did you even go to school?"

A couple of the men who'd been standing around waiting for their orders chuckled at that. Malcolm rounded on them, eyes flashing.

"You think that's funny?" he snapped. "So we bust our asses loading up this truck and then we take off where? Into the woods? Then what?"

"We talked about this," Roth sighed. "We keep going until we find where we want to settle down."

"So we're picking up weapons just so we can run." Malcolm shook his head. "What a great plan."

"We discussed—"

"No, *you* told us what we were going to do. How's that any different from what the army wants to do?"

The men all seemed to be listening intently to the conversation, even the five who were aiming their rifles at Jax and crew and the two guards.

"That's a good question," said Jax, seeing the opportunity to sow a little chaos. "Sounds like same shit, different commander to me."

Roth glowered. "Don't listen to him. We talked about this. We have the freedom to decide our own destinies. Once we're armed, we can have the confidence to make our own way. Go anywhere we want, do anything we want."

"What if we don't all want to go to the same place?" asked Malcolm. "What then?"

"We can decide later where we'll end up," said Roth. "But right now we're burning daylight. We need to get loaded up."

"I never did get that part of it," said one of the men who was guarding Stratch and Perry. "I mean, I grew up here. This is my home. I don't know if I want to leave."

Malcolm was nodding and pointing to the soldier. "Exactly my point. And no matter where we go, you can sure as shit count on one thing: there ain't gonna be a Cheyenne Mountain base there. This is the safest place in the country right now. Why do you think the fucking military chose the place?"

Several of the men nodded, seemingly agreeing with Malcolm, at least in part.

Roth was getting visibly angry. "Jesus, you men! We've been over this! We can't attack Cheyenne and take it over. It would be suicide!"

"Not if we go in through both doors! They'd be trapped inside! Like shooting fish in a barrel!"

"We'd need a hell of a lot more men, you idiot! And they'd have to be trained! And have killer instincts!" Roth rounded on his men, eyes wide. "Anyone here ever kill someone? Ever even been in a real fight? Holding guns on unarmed people is a far cry from going into battle."

"He's right," said Jax. "I've been in combat. It's a different reality. You'd all be killed."

"Well, of course *he's* gonna say that!" Malcolm cried. "Don't believe the hype!"

The other men were glancing furtively at each other. Jax got the feeling that they were all second-guessing this whole situation. But they were committed now.

"Just stick to the plan and everything will be fine!" Roth barked. "Agreed?"

The men nodded, though without much conviction.

Roth turned to Malcolm and put a hand on the holster attached to his belt. "You need to get out of here, Austin. Just get in that sports car of yours and take off."

Malcolm crossed his arms over his chest defiantly. "I'm not going anywhere. I told you, these are *my* men."

"Hey, Austin," said one of the men. "Just chill, will you? Nick is making sense. We can't go after Cheyenne."

"What *are* we gonna do then, Steve? I didn't sign on to this to go live in the fucking woods!"

Jax squeezed Hayley's hand as he realized the girl had spent close to an hour trapped in a vehicle with this maniac.

"What did we sign on for, then?" asked Steve. "If we want to run our own lives, this is the only way we're going to do it. Yeah, it's not going to be easy, but Nick's plan is solid, man. You're starting to sound crazy."

"Wasn't so crazy when it was just us, before this asshole showed up," Malcolm said, lifting his chin in Roth's direction. His pouting tone both disgusted and frightened Jax. *This* was the kid he remembered from the stand-off with the jerry can at the strip mall.

"That's it," said Roth. He drew his SIG Sauer. "This ends here. Get lost, Austin, or I'll put a bullet in you right now."

Macolm's eyes widened. He wasn't expecting this. Jax saw the potential for an opening.

"Big man with a gun," the kid said. "Put it down and we'll see who walks away from this."

"We don't have time for this!" Roth roared. "Men, show Mr. Austin we mean business."

The others shared a few glances before turning to face Malcolm, their weapons now trained on him. Jax saw his opening—he managed to catch Perry's eye and motioned for him to use the radio on his hip. Perry nodded, reaching slowly to his belt. While all eyes were on Malcolm, the guard yanked the walkie free and brought it to his mouth.

"Cheyenne, this is Schriever!" he bellowed. "Mayday mayday mayday! The stronghold has been breached, repeat, the stronghold has been breached! Capt. Booth and his team are here! A dozen hostiles—"

Before Jax could breathe, the man closest to Perry had already spun and fired his weapon. Jax watched in horror as the guard's chest exploded out his back.

"Jesus!" Roth cried. *"Stand down!"*

Hayley shrieked beside Jax as his mind raced. His first thought was to grab the AR-15 from the man closest to him, but he quickly kiboshed it; there was too much potential for him to suffer the same fate as Perry. In the end, he held his ground.

Immediately, he saw that Malcolm had the same idea. The kid grabbed the rifle from Steve, struggling to wrestle it from his grip as the rest of the men looked from Perry to Malcolm, back and forth, frozen in panic.

Jax instinctively threw Hayley to the concrete floor and covered her with his own body. Ruben and Carly hit the decks right after, landing beside him. A moment later, the air around them exploded with the sound of .223 Remington rounds flying over their heads.

"Get down!" they heard Roth yell. More gunfire followed. Jax raised his head just in time to see Malcolm Austin sprinting for the ridiculous car he'd arrived in with Hayley. His former colleagues were still firing on him, though the shots weren't even close to striking home. A few seconds later, the kid reached the car, tossed his rife in the back and jumped in. The tires shrieked like a hawk as the car sped off into the parking lot before finally disappearing into the distance, hurtling toward the sun as it sat above the western horizon.

"Hold your fire!" The authority of Roth's voice was undeniable, built up by years of command.

Jax and Ruben looked up, then at each other. The immediate threat appeared to be over. The rest of Roth's men seemed stunned by what had just happened, including their own roles in it. They blinked owlishly, gazing around the place.

Roth ran a hand down his face. "Jesus Christ," he groaned. "What a shit show."

Jax picked up Hayley and stood. She was trembling, tears streaming down her face, but unhurt. He hugged her tight, feeling her little heart racing against his chest.

"Shhh," he whispered into her hair. "It's over. We won't let anything happen to you. You're safe."

Ruben pulled Carly to her feet. As soon as she was up, she rounded on Roth, crimson blood in her pale cheeks and naked fury in her eyes.

"Look at what you've done, you bastard!" she screeched. "Just take the goddamn van and get out of here! Troops won't be here for at least a half-hour. You have enough of a head start."

Roth looked stricken. "We just killed a soldier, Carly," he said quietly. "We could have killed all of you. We're trying to steal military weapons. You think they'll slap us on the wrist and let us get away?"

"You can go in any direction," Jax growled. "They can't track you from the air. You can make it out of here easily. Just go!"

Roth shook his head. "Not without the weapons. If the army didn't have enough reason to come after us before, they sure as hell will now." He looked at his wrist, then to his men. "We have twenty minutes to get as much of this on the truck as we can, then we head out."

He looked at Jax and Ruben. "You, too." Then to Stratch. "That includes you, soldier. Double time."

The private's jaw dropped. "You just killed a man!" he cried. "Are you out of your fucking mind?"

"Quite possibly," Roth sighed. "If you don't want to join him, move it. One more dead body doesn't mean a whole hell of a lot these days. The buildings around us are full of them."

Ruben looked at Jax. "Any point in resisting?"

"No. The sooner they get out of here, the sooner this is over with."

Jax dropped to a knee beside Hayley. "Carly will look after you.

Just try to stay out of the way, okay? We have to do some work, but we'll get out of here soon and then we can go back to the mountain."

Roth appeared beside them with a length of nylon rope in his hand and an apologetic look on his face.

"Sorry," he said. "We can't risk her running around."

Ruben stepped between him and the girl. "Get the fuck out of here with that before I wrap it around your neck, asshole."

"Ruben," Jax said. "It's not worth it." He turned to Hayley. "I'm sorry, kiddo. It's only for a little while."

She gave Jax a resigned nod that kicked him straight in the guts and held out her hands. Roth wrapped the rope loosely around her tiny wrists, then secured it with a complex knot.

"I'm sorry about this," he told her.

"Blow it out your ass," she replied solemnly.

Jax felt his heart swell with pride even as Ruben stifled a laugh and Carly's eyes widened into saucers. Even Roth smiled.

"You've got a very brave girl there, Captain. The smoother things go here, the sooner you can get back to whatever lives you've managed to build here in our glorious new republic."

"Blow it out your ass," Jax said.

Roth chuckled and shook his head. Jax felt he was putting on a good show of hiding his horror at what had happened. He himself had seen death before, up close and personal. It was abundantly clear that Roth hadn't.

Twenty minutes later, the truck had forty crates of ammo, two hundred rifles, just as many pistols, four grenade launchers and two crates of shaped charges under its tarp. The forklift had lasted just long enough to get the crates on board before crapping out. Jax, Ruben and Stratch had stripped down to their T-shirts to do the work while Carly sat with Hayley.

"Good work," said Roth. "Let's get these five secured and get the fuck out of here."

Jax frowned. "What are you talking about?"

Three men with ropes approached them. "Sorry," said Roth. "You said it yourself: we can take any direction we want. I'm not going to risk the possibility that one of you will see which direction that is. Look on the bright side: the cavalry can't be more than fifteen minutes out."

He sighed. Roth had him. "Fine, just get it over with."

The men worked quickly under Roth's supervision, securing the ropes so that all the adults were bound wrist to ankle. Hayley's wrists were still tied in front of her. They weren't going anywhere any time soon.

Roth told Steve to collect the van they'd arrived in, then directed half of the men to ride with him and the others to board the transport truck.

"We're in the home stretch," he said. "We've got what we need, an open road and a head start."

Another of the men took the weapons the guards had been assigned and tossed them into the back of the truck. "That's all of it, boss."

"Have a nice life," Ruben said with a grin. "Best keep an eye in your rearview camera, just in case Jax and I ever get an urge to go on a road trip."

Roth hunkered next to where they sat on the floor, beside an office at the back of the building.

"You still don't quite get what I've been saying, do you?" he asked with a grin of his own. "There's nothing but space in America now. We don't have to run into each other ever again if we don't want to. There's a whole country out there. A little piece for everyone."

"Yeah, well, a piece of my foot will be up your ass if we ever meet again, that's all I'm saying."

"I don't think either of you have to worry about it," said a dull voice from inside the office. "Neither of you is leaving here alive."

27

Jax looked up to see Malcolm Austin standing in the office doorway. The rifle he'd stolen from one of the other men was trained on all of them, including Roth.

His instinct was to struggle with his ropes, but an instant later he knew it was pointless. He wasn't going to be able to move. Beside him, he could see Ruben coming to the same conclusion.

Roth's expression dropped as he realized who was speaking behind him. He was still crouched next to them, his back to the office. Jax looked into the room and saw the small exterior door they'd propped open to draw a breeze in while they'd worked. *Shit*, he thought with an internal groan. *Shit shit shit.*

Roth raised his hands slowly and rose from the floor, his back still to Malcolm.

"You came back," he said evenly. "How did you get in without us noticing?"

"Cool thing about the Nighthawk," said the kid. "It's got an electric mode. Nobody ever uses it, but it does. Totally silent. I've been back since you started loading the truck."

"And you didn't help?" said Ruben. "No dessert for you tonight."

"Shut up." He jerked the gun toward the center of the building. "Get over there, Nick. We're gonna have a meeting."

"It's a coup, then?" Roth said as he walked.

"A what?"

"Never mind."

Jax leaned closer to the rest of his crew. "This is bad," he whispered. "At least with Roth we were dealing with someone we could predict. I don't like the look in that kid's eyes."

"He's crazy," Hayley hissed. "You should have heard what he was talking about on the way here. About how he was going to get back at everyone who hurt him since he was a kid. He said his dad used to beat him up, and that he was glad when he got killed at the school."

"Jesus," said Carly. "Roth signed a deal with the devil when he joined forces with him."

They watched as Roth and Malcolm stopped next to the remaining weapons and ammo stacked in the center of the building. Outside the big front doors, they saw the rest of the men milling around with the van and the truck, obviously waiting on Roth.

"Guys!" Malcolm called out. "Little confab here, all right?"

"We don't have time for this shit," Roth growled as the other men wandered into the building. "The army is on its way here as we speak, you stupid little shit!"

"The fuck?" one of the other men said. "What's *he* doing here?"

"He's about to get us killed is what he's doing," said Roth. "Shoot him. Now."

Jax saw the opening he'd been waiting for: delay them until they didn't have time to get away.

"Really, Roth?" he called from their spot by the office. "You want your men to kill one of their own? Tell me how you're better than the army again. At least we feed our men."

"Shut up!" Roth barked, clearly desperate now. "We don't have time for this! Tie Austin up, knock him out, whatever it takes. Just do it and let's get out of here!"

The other men looked at each other, all of them obviously wondering who would take care of Malcolm.

"Anybody makes a move on me and Roth is done, too," the kid said. "Then you got no leader at all."

Jax wouldn't have believed what happened next if he hadn't seen it with his own eyes: Roth dropped his right hand from behind his head and knocked the barrel of Malcolm's rifle downwards, where it discharged, tearing chunks of concrete out of the floor. Roth was easily thirty years older than the kid, but he clearly remembered his training.

Unfortunately for him, Malcolm was quick as a mongoose. He recovered immediately and brought the barrel back up in an arc, hoping to position it under Roth's chin. The former colonel managed to grab it in his right fist, but the leverage was almost non-existent. Another burst of gunfire shook and heated the barrel in his hand and he cried out in shock and pain.

"Do something!" Jax heard Steve yell from the crowd. "Save him!"

"Which one?" another answered.

Jax's combat instincts kicked in as he saw Malcolm yank his weapon away from Roth. The kid overcompensated and stumbled backwards, landing hard on his ass. As he did, Jax yelled for his companions to duck as he knocked Hayley to the ground yet again with his shoulder and rolled on top of her.

Malcolm's rifle fired a burst of rounds that were close enough that Jax could swear he almost felt them. His heart thundered in his chest as he prayed to whatever gods there might be that another burst wasn't coming in their direction.

A hard *thwack* from Malcolm's direction drew Jax's attention from the floor. He looked up just in time to see the kid staggering after a blow from the stock of one of his comrades' rifles.

"Jax!" Ruben hissed from beside him. "Twelve o'clock!"

He looked above them to see what Ruben was pointing out: the bullets had torn through a metal shelf on a unit next to the wall outside the office, leaving a jagged edge on the corner. His heart leapt at the sight.

"Go!" he whispered back, and Ruben was immediately there, sawing the rope around his wrist across the metal edge, back and forth until it snapped. In those precious few seconds, Malcolm had managed to recover and was running with his rifle in their direction, firing wildly at Roth.

Once Ruben's wrists were free, Jax motioned for Carly to follow suit. She was flushed with panic but managed to do what she had to until her hands were also free. While she and Ruben untied their ankles, Jax motioned for Stratch to take his turn. Hayley, smart little soldier that she had become, stayed flat on the floor.

The warehouse was a symphony of gunfire now as Malcolm fired back at his former friends and they fired at him. The only one with any real shooting experience was Roth, and he was the only one without a weapon at the moment. The risk of them being hit by a stray bullet was strong enough that Jax motioned for his people to stay down on the floor.

"Motherfucker!" one of the men yelled. Jax looked up to see Steve clutch his right shoulder with his left hand, blood gushing from a fresh wound. He staggered to his right as Roth reached him and snatched his rifle.

Jax grabbed Hayley and pulled her into the office with him in an obstacle course crawl as the other three followed. Once inside, Jax hurried to the door that had been propped open. It was at the back of the building and so faced the opposite direction of the main doors.

The roaring gunfire inside made it hard to hear anything, but Jax could see what he'd been hoping for in the distance: three armored troop transports headed up the back way toward them.

"They're here!" he said, pulling Ruben to the door so he could see as well. "All we need to do is hunker in here until they all kill themselves out there, or the cavalry gets here. Either one is fine with me."

"There's nothing in this world as beautiful as a Gargoyle headed your way," Ruben said with a wide grin. "We might just get out of this yet."

That was when they heard the shriek.

28

They both turned to see Carly holding onto Hayley's legs as Malcolm Austin pulled her by her bound wrists with his left hand. His right was on a SIG Sauer and it was pointed at her temple.

"Let her go, you bastard!" Carly spat, but Jax knew it was a lost cause. She finally lost her grip.

Stratch stood and raised his fists. "Take *me*, tough guy!"

"Fuck off," Malcolm said absently as he hauled Hayley, twisting and screaming like a wet cat, out into the gunfire. Jax's belly was ice as he contemplated making a run for it and knocking her to the floor.

Before he could move, Malcolm was in position behind a crate. "Hold your fire!" he hollered. "I have the little girl!"

Roth held his fist up, a signal for the others to stop shooting. "She's not part of this, Austin! I'll throw my weapon to you, then you let her go! I'll be unarmed!"

Malcolm's grin made Jax's breath freeze in his chest. Whatever rudimentary intelligence might have once been behind the kid's eyes before had been replaced with sheer madness.

"Ain't gonna happen!" he cried. "She's my ticket outta here! You idiots can't see it, but the army's already here! Coming right up our tailpipe!"

Jax watched the other men scatter, looking for a way to see what was happening. Roth yelled for them to maintain position, but none of them did. Some of them took refuge behind crates as if preparing for a firefight. A couple even threw their weapons on the ground and stood there, frozen, looking like they were trying to wake themselves from a nightmare.

Roth was wild-eyed now, calling for them all to surrender. They had no other option. Jax saw the words were falling on deaf ears with Malcolm; he still thought he was going to skate out of here because he had Hayley.

As the transport vehicles got closer, Jax weighed his options frantically. He and the rest of his team were a good twenty yards from Malcolm, and there was no cover between them and him. None of them were armed. Jax could risk his life and make a run for her, try to overpower Malcolm, but the odds of success were just too low. At least Hayley was alive, and Malcolm, crazy as he was, had enough sense not to do anything drastic—yet.

"They need to know there's a hostage situation in here," Carly said from beside him. "They have to be prepared to negotiate."

It suddenly occurred to Jax that Stratch still had his walkie-talkie. He grabbed it from the private's belt and hit the button.

"Mayday mayday mayday!" he hissed into the mic. "This is Booth! They have my girl hostage, repeat, my girl is a hostage in the Schriever situation! Approach with extreme caution and be prepared for negotiations!"

He waited but there was no response. Inside the building, everyone seemed to be holding their breath. Even Malcolm simply stood there, holding a struggling Hayley in place and panting with exertion. They all seemed to be waiting to see how the army would deal with them. Jax had no doubt some of them were praying that they would have a future. He had no idea what Archer's punishment for treason would be in this new republic, but he was sure Roth wasn't in any hurry to find out. The man seemed to be searching for a window to jump out of.

"Still radio silence," said Ruben. "What the hell?"

Jax scowled. "Maybe we should tell them there's only one armed hostile left."

"Guys," said Carly.

"If they didn't answer the first time, what makes you think they'll answer a second?"

"Guys."

"We have to try," said Jax. "Whatever it takes to keep them from startling Malcolm."

"Guys!"

They turned to Carly and saw what she was seeing through the open door of the office. The three troop transports were closer now: low and wide, with three six-foot wheels and an M61 Vulcan 20-millimeter rotary cannon capable of firing a hundred rounds per second on each side. Each had a half-dozen roof-mounted Hydra 250 rockets capable of blowing through several feet of concrete. Gargoyles earned their nickname: they were hell on wheels.

And they weren't stopping.

"What the fuck..." Ruben breathed.

Carly gripped Jax's shoulder. "What are they doing?"

Jax waited for the blanket of calm that always enveloped him in combat, and again, it didn't come. But his mind didn't fail him: he was calculating at the speed of light, running scenarios, weighing odds and risks.

The answer came to him a fraction of a second before the chaos started—an answer that would have horrified him if he'd had time to think about it. But he didn't, and that likely saved all their lives.

Jax grabbed Ruben and Carly by their collars and yanked them forward with the momentum of his sprint. Stratch stood directly in front of him and was tackled along with them as Jax's legs pumped like pistons, pulling them forward and down as the Hydra 250 left its tube on the top of the lead Gargoyle and rocketed its way to the wall where they had been standing only moments earlier.

As they moved forward and down, back to the floor yet again, Jax caught sight of Hayley struggling against Malcolm. Brave little Hayley, kicking at the kid's shins and raking his hand with her nails. His mind formed a quick, intense prayer that wasn't in the form of words, but the gist of it was this: *If there's anyone listening, please let her live. If she can't live, please make it quick.*

Then the world blew up. Jax felt the Hydra's impact as pressure against his eardrums rather than actual sound. Behind them, chunks of concrete imploded into the room with enough force to drive him and his companions forward several inches along the surface of the floor. Jax felt a vague tearing sensation in his left calf but ignored it for two beats before staggering to his feet.

He knew the Gargoyle's crew would wait a handful of seconds to assess the damage before attacking again. He had only that much time to get Hayley out of the line of fire. As he stumbled forward, he could see them as grey silhouettes through the smoke and concrete dust. Malcolm was getting to his feet, still gripping her shirt in his fist.

Jax could make out more detail as he got closer: both of them were covered in dust and blood, but the barbed wire around his guts loosened a little when he saw Hayley move and heard her cough. Malcolm was working hard to keep his footing, but still he wouldn't let the girl go. And the SIG was still in his other hand.

A dozen yards away, the remainder of Roth's men were in various stages of dealing with the Hydra's effects. They were lucky they had been as far from the wall as they were when the rocket hit, but some still sported bleeding wounds. Roth himself was nowhere to be seen.

Jax registered all of this in less than a heartbeat. He also saw that Malcolm still hadn't fully regained his equilibrium, and that was his opening. He reached out and grabbed Hayley's arm, pulling her toward him until she was like a tug-o-war rope between the two men. As he did, an exquisite jolt of pain rode through his calf like lightning, and Jax dropped to one knee, leaving him with no leverage.

The dust and smoke had cleared enough for Jax to see the kid's eyes: they swam and rolled in a way that made Jax think of the time he was a teenager back in Texas and had to rescue a cow that had been trapped in the mud by a flash flood. It was mad panic.

"Let go of her!" he shouted with a desperation he'd never known before. "It's over! She can't help you anymore!"

"Then what good is she?" Malcolm asked blandly. He gave one final tug to pull her closer to him and jammed the barrel of the SIG into the hollow at the back of her skull.

The sound of the shot hit Jax like a spear to his heart.

29

Malcolm spun forward and to his left as the slug tore through his scapula and exited through the front of his deltoid muscle in a shower of blood, bone and cartilage. Hayley screamed as some of it landed in her hair. Jax thought absently that he'd never heard such a wonderful sound in his life.

The kid's now useless left hand finally let go of the girl and Jax pushed himself upright with his one good leg. As he grabbed Hayley, he saw Roth swaying some fifty feet beyond them, the stock of the AR-15 he'd shot Malcolm with still propped in his shoulder. All of it had taken place in the space of less than five seconds.

Jax limped with Hayley toward a steel storage bin that was the only solid shelter they could reach. He knew what was coming next, even if the others didn't. Meanwhile, Malcolm had managed to right himself and was slowly raising the SIG in Roth's direction. The last sight Jax saw before he pulled Hayley to him and curled the two of them into a ball was the kid's bloody teeth grinning like a jack-o-lantern's.

"Toldja we shoulda taken the fight to them," he gurgled before Roth's next shot took his head off his shoulders.

Now that he was facing towards the wall again, Jax could see what he knew was coming. The Gargoyle had moved closer and was now less than twenty yards from the hole the Hydra had blown in the wall. Now the matching pair of Vulcans were staring at them like cold eyes in the smoke and dust.

"DOOWWN!" he bellowed, not knowing if it would do anyone any good. He and Hayley were at enough of an angle that they were effectively out of range, but he had no idea where anyone else was.

The *rat-a-tat-tat* of the Vulcans echoed throughout the space as thousands of 20-millimeter rounds tore through everything in their path. Jax's hands were on Hayley's ears, leaving his own unprotected against the deafening noise. But worse—far worse—was the coldness in his soul that came from knowing that Hayley would live with the memory of this moment for the rest of her life. She'd wake up screaming years from now, reliving it, her heart galloping in her chest.

But at least she would be alive.

The staccato rap of the guns lasted an eon in Jax's mind—surely entire civilizations rose and fell in the time it took them to empty their ammunition belts, all while he held Hayley's ears and shielded her body with his. His mind's eye filled with images of Roth and his men being ripped to hamburger by the storm of gunfire.

When silence finally fell, it was like a physical force against his ears. He took a deep breath and braced himself for the pain that was about to rake his esophagus.

"HOLD YOUR FIRE!" he screamed. *"IT'S BOOTH!"*

The shout combined with the smoke and dust to give him a coughing fit. Beneath him, he could feel Hayley's body trembling with her own hacking sobs. It was awful, but it was *motion*, and motion meant she was alive.

He heard Cruz's startled voice from somewhere near the hole in the wall: "*Captain?* Holy shit, Captain, are you *in* here?" She hollered to the outside: "Hold your fire! Jesus Christ, *hold your fire!*"

Jax let out the breath he'd been holding. "Lambert and Grant are over near you!" he rasped. "Find them!"

As shouts echoed around them, he sat back and let Hayley move.

Her hair was a rat's nest, her face smeared with blood and streaks of dust and debris. Her wide eyes were damp and red-rimmed, her face pale with shock, her body trembling.

It was the most horrible, most beautiful sight he'd ever seen.

"Is it over?" she croaked.

Jax pulled her to his chest and squeezed her tight, as if he needed to make sure she was real. Then he let go and started inspecting her, turning her over and checking every inch.

"It's over," he said. "Are you all right? Does it hurt anywhere?"

"My face. I think I cut my forehead."

"Anything else?"

She shook her head. "I don't think so. Your leg is bleeding."

Jax looked down to where she was pointing and saw a gaping hole in his left calf muscle. He'd need a tourniquet, and soon, or he'd likely pass out. But it was the furthest thing from his mind right now.

Two dozen more men swarmed through the hole in the wall behind Farries, rifles at the ready. Shouts of "Clear!" echoed around them, no doubt as they recognized that any threat there might have once been was long gone. Jax would have been astounded if any of Roth's men had survived.

Cruz appeared next to them and crouched down, frantically groping Hayley for injuries.

"Oh, my girl," she whispered. "Please be okay, please be okay..."

"We're not critical," said Jax. He hawked a clot of dust from his throat and spit it onto the floor. "What about Lambert and Grant? And the guard, Stratch?"

"Same, injured but not critical. We've got a truck with us, we'll get you all back to base. Pardon my French, sir, but what the *fuck* were you doing here?"

"It's a long story." He paused a moment. "Wait a minute—base didn't tell you we were here?"

Cruz shook her head. "Our orders from Col. Smith were to attack the building with extreme prejudice first, retrieve the weapons second. No hostiles were to make it out alive."

Hostiles, Jax thought. *Fucking beer league wannabe soldiers are hostiles now.*

That wasn't the worst thing on his mind at the moment, but he would have to hold onto that for later.

Cruz helped Jax to his feet and propped him up with an arm across the shoulder. Hayley took one of Jax's hands and one of Cruz's and shuffled along beside them toward the front doors. As they passed, he noticed the girl steadfastly avoiding looking at the floor and the chewed remains of what had a few minutes ago been men. Like all children of war, she was growing up too fast.

"Motherfucker!"

The sound of the word coming out of Carly Grant's mouth startled him. A member of Echo had a hand on her elbow and another on her upper back; Jax deduced that he'd just popped a dislocated shoulder back into place.

Beside her on the floor amidst the rubble, Ruben held a wadded towel to his scalp. It was almost completely crimson, but he still managed to smile at Hayley as they approached.

"You okay, Princess?" he asked.

"Roger that," she said. Her voice was flat, but at least she was talking. Jax took that as a win.

Cpl. Farries appeared and saluted Jax. "Sir, we've radioed ahead to base. They'll have the infirmary ready for all of you."

He nodded. "Thank you, Corporal."

Should have told them to get ready to add a dozen more corpses to the pile as well, he thought, but he kept that to himself.

30

"I still don't get it," Jax said, bewildered. "The pants fit *all* of the girls, even though they're not the same size? How is that possible?"

Hayley looked at Cruz, who rolled her eyes comically. "Boys," she said. "They just don't get it."

"It's just a story, Jax," Hayley sighed. "It's not about the pants, it's about friendship."

She giggled softly, and Jax thought the sound was like music. Her resilience was downright amazing in the aftermath of everything she'd been through. Then again, he supposed, whose wasn't these days? It was amazing how quickly people's tolerance for insanity had gone up.

They were at his bedside in the infirmary the next day. He'd lost a lot of blood, though not enough to need a transfusion, and his stitched left calf looked like something off a cadaver after an autopsy. But he was on intravenous fluids, and the medic who had treated him said he'd be discharged by morning, which was all he could have hoped for.

"Are you talking about the Sisterhood books?" said a familiar voice from the doorway. It was Carly Grant, sporting a sling to hold up her damaged shoulder, but otherwise none the worse for wear. Physically, at least. Jax had no way to know how her first taste of combat had affected her soul.

"Uh-huh," Hayley grinned.

"I used to love those when I was your age!" She sat down in a chair next to Hayley and Cruz. "How's our fearless leader?"

"He'll live," said Jax.

Hayley gripped his hand. "I'll take care of him and make sure he does what he's told. You guys can't give him orders, but *I* can."

He smiled and saluted with his other hand. "Yes, ma'am."

"Speaking of orders, that's why I'm here," said Carly. "Col. Smith wants to see you as soon as you're discharged."

Jax nodded, frowning. "Good. I want to see him, too."

THE CANE TOOK a little getting used to, but it helped with the pain as he walked. Dr. Whitelaw, a civilian physician in his 80s who'd somehow managed to survive the epidemic and offered his services to the army, had warned him against painkillers.

"Dope is like land now," the doc had said. "They're not making it anymore. Sure, there's a lot of it lying around, but once it's gone, it's gone. I was in Vietnam, and I saw what happens when you run out in a really bad situation. Much as I hate to say it, if you're not screaming, you don't need it. Get my drift?"

Jax did get his drift. He'd been wounded before—he had the Purple Heart and a couple of bronze oak leaves to prove it—and he'd never taken anything after being released.

Now, as he approached Smith's office, his leg was the last thing on his mind. The door was open, so he knocked on the jamb.

"Come," Smith said without looking up from his papers. From this angle, Jax could see some silver hair creeping in on the top of his head.

"You wanted to see me, sir?"

Smith glanced at him. "Captain. Yes, come in. Close the door behind you."

Jax did as he was told and hobbled to the chair in front of Smith's desk. He winced as he lowered himself to sit.

"I read your report," Smith said in his usual monotone. "Just wanted clarity on a couple of points."

"Yessir."

"You, Lambert and Grant were abducted by Roth and his men at gunpoint, correct? Were any of you carrying your sidearms at the time?"

Jax glared at him, his hackles rising even higher than they'd already been when he walked in.

"If we had been, we obviously would have tried to use them," he said.

"Why didn't you have them?"

"It was a recruitment drive. The whole point of what we were doing was to appear less threatening so that civilians start to respect us instead of just being scared of us. Sir."

Smith nodded. "I get that, but from now on, sidearms are part of your uniform. Understood?"

"Is that from you or from Gen. Archer?"

Jax squared his jaw as Smith leaned back in his seat. It was open insubordination, and they both knew it. He didn't care; Smith was lucky Jax hadn't given in to his rage and pummeled him the second he walked in the door for putting his team—and more importantly, Hayley—into the line of fire needlessly.

Smith eyed him for several moments before speaking. "Those are *my* orders, Captain. And I expect them to be followed."

"Of course, sir. I was just wondering. Though I doubt a pistol would have helped much, considering Roth's man had already kidnapped my ward. He had me over a barrel."

"About that. This girl—"

"Her name is Hayley Moore, sir. I'm her legal guardian."

Smith's bland expression didn't change. "I doubt that, Captain.

You and her mother weren't even engaged before she died. The legal process of gaining custody takes months."

Jax's heart gave a hard thump against his chest but he kept silent.

"That means you brought her to the U.S. under false pretenses," Smith continued. "And she got an Eko inoculation that could have gone to military personnel. And she's living here at Cheyenne, even though she has no legal or family ties here whatsoever."

The two men stared at each other for several beats, neither blinking. Jax knew this was a standoff. How it would end was anyone's guess.

"Begging your pardon, sir," he said finally. "But what's your point?"

Smith leaned forward and propped his elbows on the desk between them.

"I'm saying that having this girl here is an indulgence on my part. I'll look the other way—for now—but we can't have her being used as leverage against you the way Roth did. You're the commander of Echo Company, which means you need to be beyond compromise. Am I making myself clear?"

Jax nodded. "Crystal, sir. I appreciate your sensitivity in the matter."

Smith surprised him by smiling. "I'm not an ogre, Captain, despite what some people seem to think. I understand that this is a unique situation. But Eko has left us with no shortage of orphans, and I can't be seen as giving preferential treatment. We'll play it by ear, if that works for you."

"Absolutely, sir. Thank you."

"Good. Now, unless you have something else to add, you're dismissed."

Jax grinned. "As a matter of fact, there is something I was hoping to discuss with you."

Smith glanced at his watch. "Go ahead. I've got a few minutes."

"I just wanted to get a couple of things clear in my own head about the incident at Schriever."

"All right." Smith's eyes narrowed. "I'll give you what I can."

"My men said their orders were to shoot first and ask questions later."

"Essentially. They were told to keep those weapons out of enemy hands at all costs."

Jax nodded. "Cruz said that they saw Roth's men, armed, coming and going from the building when they arrived, so she assumed they were expected to level the building and take out the enemy."

"So what part of this is unclear, Captain?"

Jax leaned forward, still maintaining a look of mild curiosity. "Pvt. Perry radioed in the situation to base while Roth and his men were in the process of loading the weapons. He was killed in the process."

Smith shrugged. "Again, what's unclear?"

"Here's the thing," Jax said, leaning back in his chair. "I was next to him when he did it, and I distinctly remember hearing him say 'Captain Booth and his team are here.' And yet when Echo arrived, Cruz said they hadn't been told about us. Just the dozen hostiles."

The colonel's face didn't betray anything.

"Obviously there was breakdown in communications somewhere along the line," Smith said evenly. "Dispatch that relayed the message must have missed that part of the transmission. Or maybe the radio cut out."

Jax nodded. "I suppose anything is possible, sir. But here's the funny thing: Perry mentioned us *before* he mentioned the number of hostiles. So somehow that part of the message got missed, even though it was right in the middle."

This time, Jax thought he saw something in Smith's eyes.

"Again," said Smith. "A breakdown in communication. When I gave my orders, I didn't know your team was in the building. It's an unfortunate oversight, but that's combat. You should know that better than anyone, Captain."

"Absolutely, sir. Nobody in this army uses the word FUBAR more than me. But there's one thing I can't reconcile here."

He made Smith wait for it again. It was petty, sure, but who cared?

"And what would that be, Captain?"

"Even if they missed part of the transmission, dispatch had to have known that Perry was in the building; he called in the situation. Which means you had to have known there was at least one soldier in there, and likely two, given that there were two men assigned to the duty."

Smith was silent for a long time. When he finally spoke, there was an undertone of anger that Jax found oddly satisfying. The guy was as cool as they came, but he did have emotions after all. Real ones, not the empty smiles.

"Just get to the point, Captain," Smith said curtly. "I don't have all day."

Jax pushed himself into a standing position and grabbed his cane.

"I just think it sounds an awful lot like the orders you gave me when we were sent in to stop the riot in Colorado Springs. You specifically told me to make sure that any supplies were given priority. I can't help but think the same orders applied to the situation at Schriever: kill the enemies, save the weapons, in that order. Fuck the personnel in the line of fire."

Smith said nothing, but his glare was ice cold. Jax took the silence as his cue to continue and leaned forward against the desk.

"I get that we don't negotiate with terrorists," he said. "Although I don't know if a dozen civilians under the loose command of a single ex-military man can be considered terrorists. But to throw the safety of loyal soldiers to the lions in the process isn't what this army is about. Never has been, and under my watch, it never will be.

"What that tells me, Colonel, is that you don't have combat experience. If you did, you wouldn't just know the phrase 'no man left behind', you'd *live* it. In this new reality we find ourselves in, we don't have the luxury of seeing casualties as numbers."

"Don't lecture me about—"

Jax's eyes narrowed as he cut him off. "I don't give a shit whether it's soldiers or civilians, friend or enemy. There's something on the order of five and a quarter *million* corpses lying around in this state alone. I don't see how adding to that is going to move this new republic forward. *Sir*."

Smith took a deep breath, let it out. Then he tented his fingers under his chin. Jax braced for the blowback he knew was coming. He was ready for anything—or so he thought.

"You make a good point," said Smith. "Duly noted."

Jax blinked stupidly. He had come in spoiling for a fight and Smith rolled over on his back, or as close as he could ever come to that. But that wasn't going to stop Jax from pushing it right to the edge. It had to be done if he and Smith were going to continue working together, and let the chips fall where they may.

"Anything else?" asked Smith. "I really do have other things on my plate."

"There is one last thing," said Jax.

"Yes?" His expression said *hurry up.*

"I know that you're not looking the other way on Hayley out of the goodness of your heart. You obviously know about my relationship with the president. In fact, I wouldn't be surprised if you'd already brought it up with him and he told you to leave it alone."

Smith's face was stone.

"Now that I know that," Jax continued, "and given the circumstances of the last couple of days, I feel I need to pass along some critical information to you."

He leaned farther forward on the desk until his face was just inches from Smith's.

"I say this knowing full well I'm risking a court martial," he hissed. "But make no mistake: if your actions ever put my daughter in the line of fire again, I will kill you, as quickly and with as little regard as you did those men in the Atlanta airport. *Sir.*"

The two men stared at each other in silence for a full ten seconds. Then Smith gave Jax his biggest surprise yet: a sincere smile.

"Duly noted, Captain," he said with a nod, leaning back in his chair. "Now get the fuck out of here before you really piss me off."

Jax decided not to push things and did as he was told.

31

Jax tried to concentrate on the book Ruben had brought him, but it was no good. He'd never been much of a reader; he preferred to move, to think, to act. Sitting and imagining what other people were doing just wasn't in his wiring. Besides, the book—*The Bourne Identity*, by Robert Ludlum—was nothing like the movie he remembered from his childhood.

He'd received a steady stream of visitors since his visit to Smith's office. He'd given Ruben and Carly some of the details of the meeting, but most of the people who stopped by just wanted to wish him a speedy recovery.

He dropped the book on the table by his bedside when he heard a knock.

"Come in."

A man in black fatigues opened the door and held it as Colton Raines walked into the room. The president nodded and the guard—a de facto Secret Service agent, Jax supposed—closed it again, leaving the two in the room alone.

Jax saluted and struggled to get to his feet without his cane, which was under his bunk.

"At ease, Captain," Raines chuckled. "Don't hurt yourself on my account."

"Sir. It's good to see you."

"And you, son. But you need to stop putting yourself in harm's way; there aren't enough of us Texans left these days. America needs all she can get."

Jax grinned. "Yessir."

Raines hitched up his slacks and took a seat on the bed by Jax's feet. "Seriously, though, that was good work the way you handled the situation with Roth and his men. That comes from Gen. Archer, as well. He tells me several people are still with us today because of your quick thinking."

"Comes with the bars on my shoulders, sir."

"No it doesn't." The president grinned. "But I'm glad you think it does. That whole thing was FUBAR, from beginning to end. I didn't know Col. Roth before, but I sure know him now. If someone of his stature can go rogue, it's a lesson to us all."

Jax considered that. *Was* Roth a rogue? He was far from crazy, and in the end, he'd saved Hayley from Malcolm Austin. For that alone, the man would have Jax's eternal gratitude, despite everything he'd done. He decided to use the opportunity in front of him to push for answers.

"What was the point of that weapons stockpile, sir? If it's not above my pay grade."

Raines shook his head. "I don't know, Jax, but I can tell you I'm going to find out. Taking over as commander-in-chief is a little like being named the CEO of a corporation: there are a lot of moving parts that you're suddenly in charge of, and it's daunting as hell. And in a situation like we're in... all I can say is it's going to take some time."

"Of course, sir. I didn't mean anything by it."

"I know you didn't. I think we're all still feeling our way here. It's early days in this, and I can't say we're even close to coming out the other side. But we're making strides. And I think you've been a big help in that."

Jax nodded. "I appreciate that, sir."

"I don't know that you do," said Raines, his eyes narrowing. "When I first got here, I was listening to some people who have some very serious opinions about where this new republic needs to be headed. And their points are valid. But the longer this goes on, the more I wonder if we don't need to start looking at things in a different way.

"Your solution about finding civilians to aid help with the graves is a perfect case in point. We could have ordered them to do it, but you saw a different way. A better way."

"It wasn't just me, sir."

Raines grinned. "All right, maybe not. But you were the point man. And I don't know if anyone's told you yet, but ever since word got out about what happened at Schriever, the number of volunteers has gone through the roof. People want to show they're not like Roth, that they're on board with what we're doing. I credit all of that to you."

Jax looked down at the bed. He had never been good at accepting praise.

"If you say so, sir."

"I do say so, and I'm going to say more. I want you to expand your team and double your recruitment efforts once you're back on your feet. We need to make hay while the sun shines, and right now, it's shining out of your ass, my boy."

Jax snorted a laugh, which started Raines chuckling, too.

"Will do, Mr. President."

"Good. And with any luck, I can keep Smith out of your hair as much as possible." He dropped a wink. "A good leader recognizes when two of his subordinates don't play well together."

"Thank you, sir." Jax wondered just how much of his meeting with Smith had made its way up the pipeline.

Raines stood and knocked on the door. The man in black opened it as the president shook Jax's hand.

"Get well soon, Captain," he said. "We need you back at work."

"Will do, sir."

"And one last thing..."

"Sir?"

The man in black handed the president a bottle wrapped in a blue skin with the words Johnny Walker embossed in silver, and Raines passed it to Jax. He recognized it as a rare vintage of the brand's scotch that normally retailed for upwards of $500 before the collapse.

The president grinned. "Stop getting your booze at 7-11, will you?"

~

"I SUPPOSE he thinks *you* did everything," Ruben said as he knocked back his scotch.

Jax refilled his friend's cup. "What the president believes is his business. It's not up to me to change his mind."

Carly took a swig directly from the bottle of Chateau Margaux she'd liberated from the hotel. Jax had seen her toss the cork in the garbage when they walked into the mess hall, so he assumed she was in for the long haul.

"Whatever," she said. "It's not like any of us is getting a raise any time soon. I just wonder what Raines and Archer and the others at the top think about what happened."

"How do you mean?" asked Jax.

"Whatever happened in the end, I don't think Nick Roth was a bad person. Misguided, obviously, but not *evil*. I know some people think he did it because he was passed over by Archer, but trust me: I knew him. He wasn't like that. There had to have been more to it."

Ruben nodded and leaned in close. "I gotta admit, I didn't disagree with everything about Roth," he said in a low voice. "I mean, Smith's maintain-control-at-any-cost attitude has already led to a lot of deaths, and now isn't the time for more death."

Jax agreed, more than Ruben could know.

Carly took another swig of wine and wiped her mouth. "And who are we to say that the military and the president even *should* be in control? Does the Constitution still apply when 99 percent of the population isn't around anymore?"

"Careful," Jax whispered. "Best keep your voice down."

Her cheeks flushed. "Sorry," she mumbled. "M'not much of a drinker."

"She's not wrong, though," said Ruben. "To question it, I mean. Look at our Special Forces motto: *De Oppresso Liber*. It means to liberate the oppressed, not *become* the damn oppressor."

Before Jax could respond, he heard a familiar voice from behind him.

"Is this a private party, or can anyone join?"

He turned to see Maggie Stubbs standing in fatigues, arms crossed over her chest. The hair that had been held in a severe bun for so long was now bobbed, hanging just above her shoulders. For the first time, Jax noticed how attractive she was.

"I was going to say army only." He grinned. "But I guess that won't keep you out anymore, will it?"

"Nope," she said, pulling up a chai beside Carly. "As of this morning, I'm Lt. Stubbs. Col. Smith said my experience deserved a commission. I think he's out of his mind, but I'm not going to tell *him* that." She grabbed an empty cup. "So fill me up with that officer hooch, my good man."

Carly scowled. "Glad I wasted four years in nursing school to become a lieutenant. Might as well have just gotten a job and waited for the end of the world."

Her three companions looked at her for a handful of seconds, then at each other. A moment later, they broke into hysterical laughter. Carly looked offended for a heartbeat, then joined in herself.

It had been that kind of week. Hell, it had been that kind of month. Sometimes you just couldn't help laughing at the collapse of society.

~

"Do you ever think about her?"

Hayley's head was warm against the crook of his shoulder as the two of them lay in her single top bunk. The rest of the women she shared the room with were out for the evening, leaving them with some time to talk before lights out.

"Your mom?" he asked. "Of course, all the time. Why do you ask?"

"I don't know," she said. "It seems like it was a long time ago that we were in Germany. So much has happened. I thought maybe you were too busy now."

He thought about the difference between kid time and adult time —how the weeks leading up to Christmas seemed like years, and how everything starts to speed up the older you get. She was experiencing things at a different pace than he was. Like the old song said, days go slow and years go fast.

"I'll never be too busy to think about Mom, kiddo. Or you."

She sighed. "Things are so different now. It's like we went to another planet or something."

"I know. But at least we still have each other."

"Yeah. There's a bunch of new kids in the school who don't have anybody."

Jax already knew that; one of his team's new priorities, in addition to finding gravediggers, was recruiting foster parents for the waves of orphaned children that were starting to emerge. It was already starting to feel like the government of this new republic, for good or bad, was well and truly underway.

"Are you going to help them?" he asked.

She turned her head to look him in the eye. Her blond hair was its usual tousled mess. "Help them?"

"Yeah. You have a lot: me and Val and Ruben and Carly. You should always help those who aren't as fortunate as you. That's why your mom was a nurse."

Jax watched the wheels turn as she thought it over.

"But how?" she asked. "What can I do to help them?"

"Make friends with them. Listen to them. I bet some of them have been really scared for a long time now."

"That's what Ms. Sidley says."

"She sounds like a smart lady. Just like your mom."

They lay there in silence a while before Hayley spoke again. When she did, her voice was small and quiet.

"I was really scared, Jax. When Malcolm got me, and in that building with—with all the shooting. I was so scared."

Jax felt his heart crack, but he did his best to keep it out of his voice. This was a new reality, and fear was a luxury that they couldn't afford, because it could too easily become a silent killer. Not just for Hayley but for everyone.

"I know you were, honey," he said, squeezing her shoulder. "And you faced your fear like a soldier. You were so tough, I asked Col. Smith if I could put you on my team."

She looked up at him. He was gratified to see her lips curl in a tiny smile.

"You did not."

"I did, but he said no. You have to stay in school. They need you there. I've got a whole team of people, but there's only one of you."

"Okay," she said with a roll of her eyes. "I guess I can stay in school, if I *have* to."

"All right," he said. "Time for lights out."

She lifted her head and he withdrew his arm, then hopped down to the floor, leaving them at roughly eye level.

"Jax?"

"Yeah?"

"I'm sort of glad that we didn't find my grandma and grandpa."

He frowned. "Why do you say that, honey?"

"Cuz they're not really my family. I mean my *family* family. That's you and everybody here. I think that's who I'm supposed to be with. Mom made it happen up in heaven."

Jax felt hot tears sting his eyes, tried to fight them without success. Years of chasing terrorists through godforsaken deserts and he never cried. Less than a month with a defenseless little girl and he was a mess.

"I think you're right," he croaked. "When you talk to her tonight, make sure you say thank you."

"You, too," she said, her own tears streaming down her cheeks.

EPILOGUE

Dylan Nguyen loved a challenge, and he had a mother of one on his hands.

He'd been recruited by a group of army folks two days earlier to help get Cheyenne Mountain's computer system back to full strength. It had been crushed by the cyber weapon that had struck right after the Eko pandemic, and Dylan had already been hard at work on it before—well, *before*.

He fidgeted absently with his wedding ring as he scanned the lines of code on the screen in the central command room. He found the project was an excellent way to keep his mind off of Michelle and his heart from sinking into what could easily become a pit. He had a purpose. A challenge. A reason to get up in the morning. So many other survivors didn't.

That reason was in front of him right now, and it made his brain itch.

"Anything new?" asked a voice from behind him.

"I don't know," he said, not taking his eyes off the green letters on the black background. "I worked on army computers in my consulting business, but these are something else. Seriously else. So I'm not sure if I'm seeing what I think I'm seeing."

His supervisor, Lt. Purcell, a middle-aged dude with a comb-over and thick glasses, took a seat beside him. They'd struck up something resembling a friendship and Dylan found him to be a good boss, if the word boss even meant anything anymore. It's not like anyone was getting paid, although there were certain perks, such as getting a house in the city once the power was back up again.

"Yeah, Cheyenne Mountain is like something out of a science fiction movie," said Purcell. "It was the nerve center of last resort for the free world for decades. There's technology here that isn't available anywhere else on Earth, at least as far as we know."

"That's why I can't figure out what this means."

Purcell leaned over him. "What are you talking about?"

"Well, I've managed to isolate the code that the cyber weapon left in the systems that it attacked—at least I think I have."

"You're not sure?"

"Well, it looks like a duck and it quacks like a duck..."

"But it's not a duck? Sorry, I don't have the same level of computer savvy as you."

Dylan grinned. "Not a lot of people do, especially now that—well, you know. Anyway, it *does* look and quack like a duck. The strange thing is that the duck is in the desert."

"Come again?" Purcell frowned.

"Just a joke. I mean, you wouldn't expect to find a duck in the desert, you'd expect to find him in a pond."

"Okaayy...?"

"So this code, which looks like a cyber weapon and quacks like a cyber weapon, didn't come from China. If I'm reading this right, it came from somewhere in the western hemisphere."

Purcell cleared his throat. "That's impossible."

"I know, which is why this is so baffling. The only thing I can figure at this point is that it's somehow picking up on the route that it took to get here. Sort of like using a connecting boarding pass at an airport to fake your point of origin."

"So what are you saying?"

Dylan leaned back in his chair and ran a hand through his coarse black hair.

"I'm saying that if I didn't know better, I'd swear that someone had done something with this code to make it look like it originated somewhere other than where it actually did."

Purcell stared over his shoulder for several seconds, which made Dylan smile. It reminded him of how his dad used to pretend to understand what he was talking about, nodding and saying "mm-hmm" even though his knowledge of computers had stalled somewhere around Windows 12.

"But you're also saying that's impossible?" asked Purcell.

"Well, nothing's impossible," said Dylan. "But it doesn't make any sense. We know that the cyber weapon started in China and spread worldwide. And without any means of connecting with other computers around the world, I can't prove or disprove the theory. So it's really pretty much moot right now."

Purcell nodded. "Your job is to get things up and running again."

"Exactly."

"There's something else you should think about."

"What's that?"

"You heard about what happened at Schriever Air Force Base last week?" Purcell asked, leaning closer and lowering his voice.

"Some of it," said Dylan. "A bunch of guys broke in to a cache of weapons and tried to steal them, right? They all ended up dead for their trouble."

"That's it in a nutshell. The army isn't keen on resistance right now, if you get my meaning."

Dylan tilted his head and raised his hands. "You're preaching to the choir, man. That's why I'm here: I want to do my part to get things moving again. To get America back, or, you know, help start the process. My grandparents came here after the Vietnam war and by the time everything—uh, collapsed, I guess—they owned a chain of convenience stores. I went to Harvard, my sister went to Stanford. This country gave us everything."

Purcell placed a hand on his shoulder. "I appreciate that, Dylan, I really do. And I think we're on the same page. You don't want to go talking about this theory to anyone else. Especially since that's just what it is: a theory."

"Of course not. I've got enough people giving me the stink-eye on the streets as it is. I try to tell them I'm not Chinese, but I guess after Marcus Chase and everything, I suppose you can't blame them."

"It's not right by any means, but it's understandable," Purcell said with a nod. "You hit the nail on the head. We're all in this together, and starting rumors is only going to take us in the wrong direction."

Dylan held out his hand for a fist bump, which Purcell awkwardly obliged.

"Amen, brutha," he said. "Consider it forgotten. I've got enough to do without heading down rabbit holes."

"Awesome." Purcell glanced at his watch. "I've got stuff to do. You okay on your own?"

Dylan grinned. It was a joke between the two, since Purcell offered next to nothing when it came to Dylan's work. He was just there because the army had this thing about the chain of command.

"Get lost," he said. "I'll catch you later."

Purcell grinned. "Do it to it, or whatever the hell I mean."

He left the room and walked into the hall that led away from the command center. As the door latched behind him, he pulled the walkie-talkie from his belt and took a quick glance to make sure he was alone. When he was sure he was, he turned the dial to a specific frequency and hit the squelch with two long blasts and then three short ones. Then he switched to a different channel.

"Go," said a voice through the receiver.

Purcell brought the microphone close to his mouth so he could speak quietly.

"We need to meet," he said. "I think we may have to kill our new chief computer tech."

That's it. For now...

Made in the USA
Middletown, DE
29 December 2018